I0831730

TYRONE M. EDDINS JR.

DONE IN THE DARK

A Novel

Scripted Visions Publishing Group

For previews of upcoming books by Tyrone Eddins Jr. and for more information about the author and Scripted Visions Publishing Group, visit: www.scriptedvisionspublishing.com

SCRIPTED VISIONS PUBLISHING GROUP
PRESENTS

DONE IN THE DARK

A Novel

By

TYRONE EDDINS JR.

SCRIPTED VISIONS PUBLISHING GROUP
LAUREL, MD

DONE IN THE DARK

2019 Scripted Visions Publishing Group First Edition

Originally published in the United States by Scripted Visions Publishing Group LLC, Laurel, MD.

ISBN: 978-0-9850666-3-5 (print edition) &
978-0-9850666-4-2 (e-book)

Visit our website:
www.scriptedvisionspublishing.com

Printed in the United States of America on acid-free paper. Cover Design: Kedi Darby

Scripted Visions Publishing Group, LLC 2011

For Deborah A. Eddins and Tina L. Eddins. Words don't exist that would allow me to accurately convey how much you both mean to me. So, I'll simply say this: thank you and I love you...

DONE IN THE DARK

For the light stolen from our eyes
and the memories heavy in our heart
For the good and evil in us all
that brings us close, yet tears us apart...
Chasing a fleeting dream
that we lost from the start...

Standing in the darkest dark
while reaching for that brightest light
Witness to unspeakable wickedness
as we dance the dance in this unending fight
Now let all spirits rest easy because...
what's done in the dark will come to the light...

PROLOGUE

"MONSTERS AND BOOGEYMEN"

ONE

He is patience...

Because he must be, for at least a little while longer. His patience will pay off. He's sure of it. After all this time, he is confident there can be just one conclusion to this story. An ending for all endings. One he has so meticulously scripted and now stands ready to execute.

And just like every good story needs a good ending, it also needs a bad guy. Especially horror stories. And that's what this is, a horror story. One full of heartbreak, sadness, and terror. A story with boogeymen who prey on the innocent and weak. A story full of wicked people who steal, kill, take, and abuse without retribution or guilt of conscience. They do this until a hero comes along and puts a stop to their evil ways.

But this is a real-life horror story with real-life monsters, and there are no heroes. There is just him and he's nobody's hero. He doesn't consider himself to be one of the bad guys, but he's more than willing to play that role because that's how he'll be able to finish this. He needs to become the thing he hates. That's what he tells himself so he'll see this through to the end.

The bad things he's planning will be done to very bad people. They are the true bad guys in this story. They are the monsters hiding in the closet and under the bed. Sharp-fanged and razor-clawed, these predators lurk in the shadows waiting to inflict their horrible brand of pain on those who are incapable of fighting back.

In this story, the monsters have gone unchecked and unpunished. They have committed evil acts and have walked away free and clear. Until now. Now their days are numbered, and he'll be the instrument of their punishment. He'll take it upon himself to right the wrongs no one else has bothered with. He will hold those responsible accountable for their crimes.

He doesn't expect anyone to understand why he's doing this. Most people aren't able to understand how it feels to have their entire life ripped apart while the world stands by and watches. How could they possibly understand what that's like? They couldn't...not unless they've experienced what he's experienced, seen what he's seen, and felt what he's felt.

So, he'll be the bad guy, for now, the lesser of two evils. And he can live with that, so long as he does what needs doing. He's waited for so long, and now he can put closure to this part of his life.

TWO

The temperature outside has dropped steadily with the setting of the sun. In the fading light, he can see his breath forming small plumes of fog as he exhales it. His fingertips have begun to go numb inside the leather gloves he wears. The same can be said for his toes, the black leather work boots on his feet offering little in the way of warmth after standing outside for so long.

He's been waiting in this same spot for at least two hours, maybe more. But, in the end, it will be well worth the wait. He's been waiting almost a lifetime, so a few more hours won't hurt.

He places his hands inside the pockets of his gray bomber jacket, the fingers of his right hand finding and gripping the handle of the small pistol he carries. He doesn't expect to use the weapon tonight, but it reassures him to know that he has it with him. Just in case.

After another forty-five minutes, he sees what he's been waiting on. Across the street from where he's standing, two white men, both big and bulky, walk out of the front entrance of a building and get into a silver four-door sedan. A police-issued, unmarked cruiser. The alley where he's been waiting offers him enough cover so he can see them while remaining hidden from their view. Not that they would be looking for him anyway. These two have grown careless and lazy.

As he watches the men, the fire begins to burn inside of him again. Sometimes it simmers, but at times like these, whenever he is so close to retribution that he can taste it, the fire burns brightest. He's studied these two men for years, learning their lives inside and out, and today's watch has helped him put the final pieces in place.

He has their routine down to a science. He knows where they live and work, where they eat and drink, and now where they do their dirt. He is ready. He watches as the sedan pulls away from the curb, heads down the empty street, turns a corner and then fades from view. He wanted nothing more than to walk up to the driver's side of the car and empty his gun's clip into both men, ending their lives right then and there. But he couldn't do that. Not yet, but soon. He just needs the right opening. Until that opening comes, he'll remain in the shadows, watching and planning, waiting to inflict the hurt he's been holding onto for so long...

He is patience... but he is also pain...

PART ONE

"GONE"

CHAPTER 1

Washington, D.C. – circa the mid-1990s…

Beanie was gonna catch hell this time. He didn't see any way out of it. He'd messed around one too many times, and now he found himself about to get in deep trouble. He and his brother were supposed to be home almost an hour ago, but here they were still out in these streets. And, as usual, it was all his fault.

It was late in the day now and the afternoon had turned into evening. For most of the day, the sun had played hide-and-seek behind a thick cover of gray clouds. Now, it was well into its end-of-the-day retreat towards the horizon. It would be dark in just a little while, and the boys were still a few blocks from home. Beanie knew they weren't supposed to be out after dark.

If their mom hadn't started calling the house phone yet, she would soon. And when she did, they had better be in the house to answer or his parents would be pissed. If that happened, his dad would most likely kick his ass, take his Nintendo away, and not let him hang out with his homeboys for the next week or two, or maybe even three. Three whole weeks on punishment. Beanie couldn't imagine it. And he didn't even want to think about the holidays.

Christmas was a month away and with the way his grades had slipped during the last quarter, he couldn't afford to get in any more trouble. If he did, he might not get anything at all except a few pairs of socks or something like that. Maybe an ugly sweater, too. Not cool.

The thought of punishment and no presents under the tree lit a fire under Beanie, and he wanted to sprint the rest of the way home. But he couldn't just leave his brother behind. He was the oldest and his baby brother was his responsibility.

"Come on, Scoop," he called over his shoulder when he saw that his brother had lagged far behind him. "Hurry up, man."

Beanie couldn't run home, but he could at least pick up the pace. He hefted his book bag and gym bag higher up on his shoulders and began walking faster. He covered ground easier than Scoop, who was struggling to keep up on his shorter legs with his own book bag slowing him down.

Both boys were small for their ages. Beanie was eleven, but with his short, skinny frame, most people thought he was much younger. And Scoop, at just seven years old, was a shorter version of his older brother, sharing the same small build, cocoa-hued skin, and short, low-cut fade haircut. People always told them that they looked like twins and that they both would be so handsome when they grew up.

After school had let out for the day, Beanie disobeyed his parents' instructions to pick up his little brother and go straight home. They got on him about it so much that he had their speeches memorized by now. But Beanie being Beanie, always hardheaded and wanting to be slick, had hung out anyway.

He'd been unable to resist kicking it with the fellas for a bit and getting in a few runs on his school's new outdoor basketball court. He'd gone way over the thirty minutes that he'd planned on staying, making him late in picking up his little brother.

Scoop's school was at the edge of their ward's school zone, so it made for a long walk to pick him up and a much longer walk home. They could catch a couple of metro buses and make it home sooner, but Beanie liked to pocket the bus money that their parents left for them each morning.

Normally, his hustle worked if he stayed on top of his game. He got to keep the bus money and they still made it home on time. He usually skipped lunch and waited until he got home to eat, so he was able to pocket that money as well. The bus money combined with his lunch money always left him with a nice weekly stash to spend on whatever he wanted.

Scoop never gave him any trouble about them not catching the bus. His little brother preferred when they walked home because sometimes, they were able to stop at the store to grab a snack on the way. If Beanie left school on time, picked up Scoop, and they went straight home after making a quick stop at the store, it was all good. But today, like too many other days, Beanie wasn't on top of his game, and now they were rushing to get home before their parents started looking for them.

"Scoop," he called out to his little brother again. "Come on lil' bro, pick up the pace. You know we gotta get home, man. "

"Wait up, Beanie," Scoop called back to him. He sounded out of breath, and Beanie heard him coughing a little bit. The November air was chilly and wet, and it had a bite to it. Beanie hoped his brother wasn't coming down with something.

"Beanie, I'm tired and thirsty, man. Can we stop at Mr. Sam's store for a soda?"

"Nah, lil' man, we can't stop for snacks today. Remember Mom said we gotta have the house cleaned up and our homework is done by the time they get home. Plus, you know she don't like us to have all that sugar no way."

"Oh," Scoop said, "well we can just stop for a few minutes, right? I want some cupcakes. My favorite yellow ones, man."

Beanie knew what was coming. His baby brother didn't care about them being late when it came to him getting what he wanted. He didn't care if his parents found out that they always walked home instead of catching the bus. Scoop didn't care about any of that when it came to his sweet tooth. Especially since Beanie would be the one who got in trouble because he was the oldest.

He turned to face his little brother, who had already stopped walking. His eyes had narrowed into small slits and his round cheeks had spread into a wide smile.

"Come on, Beanie," Scoop said, rubbing his hands together. "I just want to get one thing. *Pleeaassee*?? Just one little thing. I'm extra hungry today. Can't you hear my tummy growlin' over here?"

"Didn't you eat lunch?" Beanie asked. "You ate your lunch today, right?"

Scoop hesitated before answering. "Well, yeah, but it wasn't any good, man," he said and threw his little arms up in the air. "I ate it, but I didn't like it much."

"Oh, yeah?" Beanie said. "And, why not?"

"Well, all I had was a sandwich and some carrot sticks and my juice box. Plus, I didn't have a treat today. *Annnd*, you had me waiting all long after school for you again, and now I'm starvin' like Marvin out here in these streets!" He placed his small gloved hands on his stomach to help emphasize his point.

Beanie wanted to laugh at his baby brother. He was almost tempted to make a detour to the store, but he knew they didn't have time for that today.

Scoop would get in there, not be able to choose what he wanted, and they would be in Mr. Sam's store all day. Then, they would be really late getting home. They wouldn't finish their chores and homework, their parents would find out what Beanie had been up to, and then it would be all over for him. There's no telling what their parents would do to him. He may not get off punishment until he turned 18 if he lived that long.

No way. He wasn't getting in trouble over his baby brother's sweet tooth. Beanie had plans to hang out this weekend, maybe even hop a bus downtown and see if he could sneak into a Hoyas game with the fellas.

"Look, buddy, I'm sorry I was late again, but we can't stop today, ok? Can't do it, man. Mom and Dad will get on our asses if we don't handle our business."

A look of disapproval flashed across Scoop's face, and the smaller boy shook his head at his older brother.

"What's up?" Beanie asked.

"You said a bad word, Beanie," Scoop said, his voice shrinking into a whisper. "Not supposed to curse."

Beanie thought about what he'd said, and he knelt in front of his kid brother. He zipped up the little guy's coat, adjusted his hat, and rubbed the top of his head.

"Sorry, buddy. You right, I shouldn't curse n' shit. I mean stuff. Damn, my bad, Scoop. Look, I shouldn't say those words, ok? But I don't want us to get in trouble. So, we gotta get home and we can't stop today, cool?"

His brother crossed his arms and opened his mouth to protest, but Beanie held up a hand to cut him off. "But...check it out, lil' man. If you work with me and help keep us out of trouble, I'll hook you up with a pack of cupcakes, *and* I'll even let you get down on my Nintendo for a whole hour this weekend. Any game you want."

Scoop's eyes lit up and he clapped his hands, but then his eyes reverted back to shrewd slits and he crossed his arms again. "Four packs of cupcakes, and four hours on your Nintendo, and ten dollars!" He held up the four fingers on his small right hand to illustrate his point.

"Four hours? Ten dollars?" Beanie said. "Man, you trippin'. No way. How about a pack of cupcakes and two hours on my Nintendo? You can even chill on my bed while you play, alright?"

Scoop considered this for a minute, even rubbing his chin and looking up at the sky for effect. "Ok, Beanie. Three packs of cupcakes, and three hours, and ten dollars."

"Two and two. Two packs of cupcakes and two hours on the video game. And five dollars. That's it. Take that or I drag you home right now kickin' and screamin'."

Scoop didn't hesitate at this offer. "Deal!" he said and stuck out his right hand. "Nice doing business with you, Big Bro!"

"Yeah, yeah, yeah," Beanie said and playfully slapped his little brother's hand. "Right. Now let's get home, you lil' hustla. You ain't supposed to scam ya big brother, ya know?"

They started walking again. Scoop was doing a much better job of keeping up now, riding high and feeling good about his new deal. Beanie was just happy to have avoided one of Scoop's temper-tantrums.

There was a little bit of daylight left in the sky, so they still had a chance to make it home before dark. Beanie would knock out the dishes, Scoop would vacuum, they would both get on their homework, and it would be all good. And all it cost him was a couple of packs of Hostess cupcakes, a couple of hours on his Nintendo, and five dollars. Not bad. He could deal with that. *Maybe he should start bribing Scoop more if it meant he could-*

The loud chirp of a police siren interrupted Beanie's thoughts. He turned and saw a brown car creeping along behind them.

"Who's that, Beanie?" Scoop asked.

"I think it's the police, man. Dunno what they want though. Come on. We gotta get home," Beanie said and tugged at Scoop's sleeve to keep him moving.

The car pulled up beside the two boys and slowed enough to keep pace with them. Whoever was inside chirped the car's siren again, and Beanie and his little brother took another couple of steps. The cruiser's tinted passenger side window lowered and revealed two men Beanie didn't recognize. He glanced over at the men but then turned away. He placed his right hand on Scoop's back and nudged him along.

"Yo, homeboys!" the man in the passenger side seat said, showing them a toothy, predatory grin as he leaned out the window. He looked like a wolf eyeing a couple of stray lambs. "Didn't you fellas hear the siren? In case you didn't know, that means stop. S-T-O-P! You boys *can* hear and you *can* spell, right?"

Beanie stopped walking and placed himself between Scoop and the car. He turned and looked at the man again but didn't answer.

The car came to a stop when the boys did, and the man in the passenger seat looked them up and down. He was a clean-faced white dude with brown hair and blue, shifty eyes. Beanie could see that something was off about him. He couldn't see the driver as clearly, but from where Beanie stood, the man behind the wheel looked like a big black dude.

"Where you boys headed?" the man in the passenger side said. "Gettin' to be a little late, isn't it?"

"Home," Beanie said, placing a protective arm around his brother's shoulder. "We're goin' home."

"Home, huh?" the man said. "And where's that?"

"Right up the block," Beanie said and pointed up the street. "Our parents are waitin' on us."

Their home was just over the next hill and Beanie wished that he and Scoop had gone straight home today. If they had gone straight home, they wouldn't be out here now getting sweated by the police.

Beanie guessed that these two dudes were cops. Had to be. They looked and sounded like cops to him and their car had a siren. Besides, who else would stop two little kids around here and mess with them for no reason?

The man looked towards the direction that Beanie had pointed and then returned his hard stare to the boys. "And where are you two lil' bastards comin' from this late?"

"School," Beanie said.

"School?" the man said and looked over at his partner. "You hear that bullshit, Slick? That a joke or what?"

The two men shared a laugh, but Beanie was sure no one had told a joke.

"Son, don't try to play us. School's been out for a couple hours now. So, why don't you tell us the truth about where you two are comin' from?"

"Already told you, officer," Beanie said as he tried, but failed, to put a hard edge in his voice. "Comin' from school."

Beanie wasn't scared of the police, but he'd learned not to trust them and to avoid them whenever possible.

"It's detective, son. And my partner and I don't like your tone, and we don't believe that shit you talkin'. So how about you stop jerkin' us around and give it up. Let's do this easy like, ok?"

"Give what up?" Beanie said, stepping backward as the man exited the vehicle and stepped onto the curb in front of them. He was a big man with broad shoulders and large, muscular arms. "I already told you, we're goin' home."

"So, you ain't out here dealing on these corners?" the man said. He was wearing faded blue jeans and a tight black sweatshirt. A shiny gold badge dangled from a chain hanging around his thick neck.

Beanie looked up at the man and shook his head.

"Well, we think maybe you are. Think you and your runner here decided the block was too hot today, so you're headin' home early. Or maybe there wasn't enough action out here. Either way, I guess you thought you could cut out without having to pay the piper?"

The cop crossed his arms across his wide chest, and Beanie could see his pistol peeking from beneath the bottom of his shirt.

"We ain't dealin'," Beanie said, his voice cracking with fear. He was for sure scared now. All he wanted was to get him and Scoop home safely. "We just comin' from school and we gotta get home."

With surprising speed, the huge man stepped forward and grabbed Beanie by his coat, snatching him forward and lifting him off his feet. "You think this is a game, boy?"

He pulled Beanie close and got right in his face. So close that Beanie could smell the cop's hot, liquor-laced breath. "Well, I got news for you. Ain't no games out here. We know you know something about the traffic on this block. Now get your skinny ass up against the car."

The cop lowered Beanie to the ground and shoved him hard against the side of his vehicle. Beanie knew he was in for a shakedown and a beatdown at least. He hoped that was all. They would find his money and take it for themselves. They would also knock him around some and then hopefully when they got bored, they would let him go. All of this because these cops were itching for a fight and had no one else to victimize right now. He and Scoop were just in the wrong place at the wrong time.

He looked over his shoulder at his little brother. He was standing just a few feet away, unmoving, his eyes as big as saucers and filled with tears, his mouth hanging wide open.

"Go home, Scoop. Get outta here. Go next door to Ms. Alice and wait for me."

Scoop didn't hesitate and took off running up the street as fast as his small legs would carry him. The cop's partner jumped out of their vehicle and started to run after Scoop. He was almost as big as the first cop and wore the same blue jeans and black sweatshirt.

"Come on, man. Let my brother go," Beanie yelled as the first cop held him in place. "He ain't got nothin' to do with any of this."

The man continued after his brother, but his partner called him back. "Don't bother, Slick. Let that lil' shit go. This punk here will do just fine."

CHAPTER 2

Scoop ran about half a block before he stopped and looked back. His chest was heaving and his nose was running. His knapsack felt like a bag of rocks now, and his heavy winter clothes felt damp with sweat.

He hadn't made it all the way up the hill and when he turned around, he saw his older brother being slammed against the hood of the brown car. The big white cop patted Beanie down, cuffed him, and pushed him into the back of his vehicle. He picked up Beanie's bags and tossed them in the car's trunk. Then the cop smiled and waved at Scoop as he got back into the car's passenger side. Scoop watched as the police cruiser pulled away from the curb, made a U-turn and sped off down the block and out of sight.

Tears began streaming down Scoop's face and heavy sobs rose in his chest. He stood there on that street corner, unsure of what to do, waiting to see if his big brother came back.

When it became clear that Beanie wasn't coming back, Scoop walked the rest of the way home. It was dark by then, but as he walked up the stairs to their apartment building, he could see that his parents were home. Their green Honda Civic was parked in one of the parking spots in front of their building.

He knocked on the door of their apartment. After a few seconds, his father snatched it open and pulled Scoop inside. His mother was right on his father's heels, and they both shouted frantic questions at him.

Where have you been? Are you ok? Why didn't you call us? Where is your brother? Where's Beanie? Do you know how much trouble you two are in? What happened? Where's your brother?? Where's Beanie? Why isn't he with you? Did he leave you? Where is he, Scoop??

Scoop didn't answer them at first. He couldn't. His voice had abandoned him. He didn't know how to put what he'd seen into words. Scoop's vision blurred and his parents' words became nothing more than muffled background noise. He stood there, a frightened little boy, staring up at his parents as he felt the hot tears welling up in his eyes again.

This made his parents more agitated. They could tell that something was very wrong and that something very bad had happened. His father's eyes grew big and he grabbed Scoop by his small shoulders and shook him some, pleading with him to answer their questions.

His mother had tears of her own streaming down her cheeks now, as she paced in a circle wringing her hands and saying, "Oh my God, Jesus Lord, something is wrong. *Scoopy, please tell us what happened!"*

After what seemed like forever, Scoop's vision cleared and his parents' pleas sounded like words again. He felt like he could talk. He looked at his parents and said, "Mommy, Daddy, they took him. They took Beanie. H-he's gone."

Scoop did his best to tell his parents exactly what had happened to him and his brother. His words forced his parents into panicked action. His dad ran out of the house looking for Beanie while his mother called the police. She sounded like she was on the verge of hysteria as she gave the police operator Beanie's name, age, and physical appearance along with Scoop's vague description of Beanie's abductors. She made sure to include the fact that at least one of the two men had identified himself as a "detective."

Scoop's father returned shortly after his mother finished talking to the police. He hadn't found Beanie or any sign of him. They had started grilling Scoop again when someone knocked on the front door. Scoop's father ran to the door and yanked it open. On the other side stood two men, one of whom wore a policeman's uniform. The other held up a badge for Scoop's father to examine. The three men spoke briefly and then his father opened the apartment door wider so the men could step inside.

The first man, a short, balding black man with a medium complexion, wore a dark gry suit and identified himself as Detective Phil Brinson from the MPD's Youth and Family Services division. The other man, a tall, young Latino named Ben Cruz, was a uniformed patrolman assigned to the same division.

The detective interviewed Scoop and his parents, scribbling the details into his notepad, while the patrolman searched the local area for any sign of Beanie. A sketch artist arrived a few minutes later, but Scoop hadn't been able to tell him much more than the race and general size of the two men who had taken his brother.

The detective acted as if he didn't believe Scoop's story. He asked questions about the places where Beanie liked to hang out, why they were leaving school so late, and if he'd ever run away before today. He said they would need more information and may need to speak to Scoop again. He also said he was sure the two men hadn't been police, but probably just a couple of thugs pretending to be police. The detective promised to try and find Beanie, but Scoop didn't believe they would do anything to help his brother.

After the policemen and the sketch artist left the apartment, Scoop's father gathered up a couple of his drinking buddies. They searched for Beanie well into the early morning hours, but they didn't find him.

His mom called everyone she could think of, crying as she asked about the whereabouts of her oldest child. No one she called had seen Beanie. Scoop couldn't remember ever seeing his mother cry this much, at least not since his grandmother had died a couple of years back.

The men that had taken Beanie said they were policemen, but policemen were supposed to protect people, right? But these men weren't interested in protecting anyone. Seemed like all they wanted to do was hurt people. Where was the protection for Beanie? Where was he right now? Was he ok? What were those men doing to him? Scoop wondered if he would ever see his brother again.

CHAPTER 3

Beanie never figured on this. He understood now that he was in a whole lot more trouble than he'd originally thought. But, the thing about it was that he hadn't done anything wrong. Not as far as he could see. He was just walking home from school with his little brother. That's it. Now he found himself in the back of a police car being taken to who knows where. Why had the police picked him up? Were these men even police? He didn't know. Beanie supposed it didn't matter because he'd been taught that even the police could be bad. He remembered hearing his parents talk many times about their mistrust of the police. His father's words echoed in his ear then: *"Police don't need no reason. If they wanna put something on you, they put it on you. Innocent or guilty don't matter in their world."* Was that what was happening to Beanie now? Were these men putting a crime on him? Were they taking him to jail?

The car sped along and seemed to catch each and every bump and pothole along the way, causing Beanie to slide back and forth across the car's backseat. His wrists had been forced behind his back and they began to ache in the tight grip of the handcuffs. The two men had not said a word since they put him in the back of their car.

Beanie had watched the buildings and houses he'd known all of his life fade away as he was taken away from his neighborhood. Not too long after they left his neighborhood, the cop in the passenger seat placed a thick black hood over Beanie's face. Now he couldn't see anything but blackness. He had no clue where he was or where he was going.

The inside of the car felt like it was a hundred degrees. Beanie felt beads of sweat roll down the back of his neck and back before they soaked into his shirt. After almost thirty minutes of bumping and swerving, the car took a sharp turn, causing Beanie to slide across the seat once again and slam hard into the car door. He fell forward in his seat as the car skidded to a sudden stop. The hood was snatched off of Beanie's head and the darkness transformed into a dimly lit room that Beanie didn't recognize. As his vision cleared, Beanie could see that he was in some sort of garage. The man in the passenger seat exited the car and disappeared through a door leading out of the garage.

"What's this, man?" Beanie said, his voice cracking with fear. "What y'all doin'? This don't look like no police station."

"Shut up," the man in the driver's seat said without looking back at him, "Keep ya damn mouth shut."

After a few minutes, the other man reappeared and gave a thumbs up sign. The driver turned off the car's ignition and turned off the car's headlights. The second man came around to the side where Beanie was sitting and opened the car's door. Without speaking, the big white man grabbed Beanie by the front of his coat and yanked him out of the car.

"Get ya ass out," the man said, "Let's go. Move it."

"What y'all doin', man?" Beanie asked again, "Where y'all taking me?"

"Move, shithead," the white dude said and gave Beanie a shove from behind. "We got a surprise for you."

The way the man said "surprise" gave Beanie a chill that ran from the back of his head to the heels of his feet.

"Make sure everything is tight, Slick," the man called back to his partner as he forced Beanie up a nearby stairwell.

"Gotcha, man," his partner replied as he exited the vehicle.

At the top of the stairs, Beanie was pushed into a small room that smelled like the locker room at his school. The room's poor lighting came from a single window that sat high up on the room's rear wall. Much too high for him to reach. There were no chairs or anything else he could stand on to try and reach the window. The room was empty except for a twin-sized mattress that sat on the floor in the back corner.

The man gave Beanie another rough shove, causing him to fall and land hard on the room's dusty wood floor. He didn't bother to remove the handcuffs. Instead, the man backed out of the room and closed the door behind him. Beanie heard a loud click as the man locked the door. All alone now and in this strange place, a new level of fear consumed Beanie. He'd thought he was too old to cry; he wasn't no baby. But right now, crying was all he could do.

I just wanna go home. I wanna go home. Please just let me go home.

After a few minutes, Beanie heard the men talking on the other side of the door. He managed to find the courage to scoot towards the door to better hear their conversation.

"Yeah, yeah man, I just talked to them while you were taking care of the car." Beanie heard one of the men say. It sounded like the white dude. "Yup, just now. It's all good. They said they got the money. Yeah, for real. All of it. Just like the last time."

"How long?" Beanie heard the black guy ask. "We can't wait all day on this one. You know people gonna be looking for this kid."

"Shouldn't be long. Day or two max. Plan is we keep the kid till then. Then we make the drop-off and collect our payday. Easy money, Slick. Good money, too."

"Not so easy, Mayday. And not so good. You know it ain't."

"Bro, come on, man. We both need this right? Hell, I know I do. I got bills and some other shit to cover. Car need brakes and baby need new shoes, man. And I know you need it too, right? The OT dried up months ago. So, we both need this lil' taste to help get our nut up until things get better."

The other man grunted in response.

"Don't sweat it, man. This is just a temporary hit until the next big case gives us them extra hours, ya know? 'Sides, man, we don't know this kid. Hell, he'll probably grow up to be a dealer or a banger anyway. Might already be one. So, just look at it like we're doing our job here. Just in a different way. Public service. Protect and serve and all that. Cleaning the streets of the bad guys and even the future bad guys."

"Yeah, I hear you, man. I hear you."

"Cool. Now, like I said, we keep the kid here for a day or two. I'll take the first shift with him while you check around, make sure no one saw anything. If you come across anything, take care of it. A couple of days, the dust clears some, we make the drop-off and we get paid, man."

"What about the other kid? The one that ran off?"

Beanie knew they were talking about his little brother. He hoped Scoop had made it home ok. Had he told their parents what happened? Were they looking for him right now? Beanie had no clue where he was, so how would they find him?

Beanie heard the white guy let out a loud laugh before he said, "Shit. No need to worry about him. You see the way he hauled ass up the block? No way he IDs us. No way in hell. Matter of fact, I doubt he remembers anything about us. And even if he does, he'll be too scared to speak up. But who knows, maybe he remembers us and maybe he looks us up when he's old enough, right?

He heard both of the men laugh this time and he shrunk away from the door. Beanie felt small. Smaller than ever. But not quite small enough. He wanted to disappear, but there was nowhere for him to go. He moved towards the back of the small room and sat awkwardly on the lumpy mattress. It smelled musty, like his gym bag when he forgot to take his sweaty gym clothes and shoes out of it after school. He thought he might know what the men were going to do with him, and it wasn't good. As he thought about what could happen to him, he fell back on the dirty mattress, brought his knees up to his chest, and closed his eyes tight as the tears started falling again.

When Beanie opened his eyes, the little bit of light that had been in the room was completely gone and he found himself staring into a sea of pitch-black. He'd cried himself to sleep, but he had no idea how much time had passed. His arms were still cuffed behind his back, and his wrists were hurting now. His throat was dry, and he wished he could have a drink of water, soda, or some Gatorade.

"Hello?" Beanie called out. "Is anyone out there?"

He listened but didn't hear an answer to his question.

"Hey!" Beanie called out again. "I said, is anyone out there?"

When he still didn't receive an answer, he started to stand up off the bed. He froze when he heard the door being unlocked and then opened.

"About time you woke up," he heard the voice of one of the men say. Beanie was sure it was the white dude he was hearing.

"You hungry?" the man asked. "Thirsty?"

Beanie hesitated but then answered, "Yeah, I'm thirsty and I gotta pee."

"I'll get you a soda or something, and I'll get you a bucket to piss in, alright?"

Beanie didn't answer. He heard the door close and lock again. A few minutes later, he heard the man return. He unlocked and opened the door and stepped inside the room. This time Beanie could see him because the man carried a small lantern and a small blue bucket in his right hand. In his left hand, the man carried a bottle of soda. Grape by the look of it. Grape soda wasn't Beanie's favorite flavor; he liked strawberry the best.

The man sat the lamp and the bucket on the floor near the front of the room and closed the door behind him. He pulled a straw from his jeans' back pocket and unwrapped it. He unscrewed the cap on the bottle and placed the straw in the soda. The man placed the tip of the straw to Beanie's lips and he took a long pull. The soda was warm and flat, but right now, it tasted as good as anything Beanie had ever had.

"Better?" the man asked when Beanie was finished drinking. Beanie nodded but remained silent. The man stood over him and looked like a giant to Beanie.

"What do you say?" the man asked.

"T-thank you," Beanie answered, but he kept his eyes on the floor to avoid looking at the man.

"What's your name, son?"

Beanie didn't want to answer, but he didn't see that he had any other choice. "Beanie. My name is Beanie."

"Beanie, huh? What's that, a nickname, boy? Ok, Beanie. You know why you're here?"

Beanie shook his head. He knew he shouldn't talk about what he'd overheard the men saying earlier.

"Good, that's good," the man said. He stepped back from the mattress and sat the plastic bottle on the dirty floor.

"Where am I?" Beanie found the courage to ask.

"Far, far away," the man said, a blank expression on his face. "No one knows you're here."

"W-when can I go home?" Beanie asked, looking up at the man, then, "I wanna go home."

"Oh, you don't need to worry about going home, little man. Matter of fact, we're going to find you a new home. How's that sound?"

"But...I don't want a new home," Beanie said, feeling like he would start crying again. "I wanna go to my home."

"Well, like I said, son," the man said, taking a step towards Beanie, "No need to worry about that right now. How about we get those cuffs off?"

Beanie's wrists were sore, but he didn't answer. Fear held his tongue and silenced his voice.

The man took a knee in front of him. He ran a rough finger across Beanie's cheek and then he cupped his chin in his large hand and squeezed hard. Beanie let loose a muffled cry from the pain.

"Yeah," the man said and licked his lips, "yeah that's nice right there." He released Beanie's chin and rubbed the top of his head and then the back of Beanie's neck before he stood to his full height.

"I'll tell you what, lil' man," he said. "Why don't we have some fun?"

"Fun?" Beanie asked, his voice low and shaky. "What kind of fun?"

"The good kind. We're gonna play a game I like. You'll like it too, I bet."

"C-can I go home after we play?" Beanie asked.

The man didn't answer. Instead, he looked Beanie up and down and then a wicked grin spread across the man's face. He pulled a small key from his pants front pocket, which he held up for Beanie to see.

"Yeah," the man said. "We're gonna have us a good time."

Beanie didn't like the sound of that. He watched the man as he stood there, his face tinted in a yellow-orange glow from the small lamp in the corner of the room. Malice burned in the man's evil eyes.

"Good time," the man repeated as he unbuttoned the front of his shirt, undid his belt buckle, and unfastened his pants.

Beanie remembered the bedtime stories he'd heard and the scary movies he'd watched growing up but had never believed. Until now. Here in this dark room with nowhere to run or hide, Beanie was sure the stories were true and that the Boogeyman was real.

CHAPTER 4

Slick drove back towards the city, intent on following his partner's orders. He steered the car north on Maryland Route 210, a long strip of multi-lane highway surrounded on both sides by woods and a few businesses and residential areas. Indian Head Highway, as it was more commonly known, was a busy stretch of road that led to and from the city and cut through multiple counties in southern Maryland. Route 210 had very few stoplights, but what it did have was a bad reputation for horrific traffic accidents due to its large volume of traffic and its appeal to street racers and drunk drivers.

Slick ignored this fact as he raced up the road, pushing the car's speedometer past 80 as he changed lanes and weaved in and out of traffic. He wanted to get to the city, do what needed doing, and then get out so he could get back to the warehouse as soon as possible. He had a bad feeling about leaving his partner alone with that kid.

Slick's right hand shook as he lifted a plastic bottle of water to his lips. He took a long drink from the bottle almost emptying it, but his throat still felt as dry as sandpaper. His stomach had knotted up and was doing flip-flops. A dull ache began to throb behind his eyes and around his temples. The beginnings of a bad headache. *What had they done? What were they doing?*

He wasn't a saint, but he was police and what they were doing now made him feel twisted and dirty. They had stashed the kid in a small, rundown warehouse deep in Waldorf, Maryland about 30-40 minutes south of D.C. They had used this location many times before for anything from beating the shit out of a suspect to screwing a couple of broads they had picked up somewhere. And they would use it again, but this time felt different to him. It felt all wrong.

Slick and Mayday had pulled jobs before and for them, the end always justified the means. But now they were moving in a direction that was becoming hard to stomach. Robbing drug dealers, shaking down wannabe gangsters. He could deal with that. Hell, he even liked it if he was being honest. He didn't even mind the few bodies they had dumped in the Anacostia or buried deep in the woods. But now they were messing with kids. They were going too far and the thought of it made Slick sick to his stomach.

The last few jobs had involved them snatching kids, driving them far away, dropping them off to someone they didn't know, and then getting paid large sums of money. *They were selling kids.* Is that what Slick had become? A human trafficker? He didn't even know how they had gotten involved in this mess. As usual, he'd been following Mayday's lead.

They were using some connection that Mayday had from his dealings in the underworld. Connections that Slick knew nothing about despite his almost decade-long friendship and partnership with Mayday. At first, Slick hadn't wanted to know the details of what they were doing, he just needed the paydays. But his mind betrayed him, and his thoughts often drifted to the kids they had taken and sold. What was happening to those innocent children? What horrors had he and Mayday condemned them to? What if someone snatched and sold his children? The kind of filth that Slick felt on his skin now didn't wash away in a shower; regardless of how long he stayed in there, regardless of how hot he made the water.

His partner rationalized what they were doing by saying they were taking kids out of bad homes and putting them with better families. He even tried to play the reform card by saying they were doing these kids a favor, a service even, by taking them out of disadvantaged situations where they would end up in jail, on drugs, or dead, and giving them a new start. Slick knew all of that was bullshit. Mayday didn't care about those kids or their welfare. Slick wasn't an idiot, but he went along with it because the money was good. Damn good. And he needed every cent of it. His financial needs exceeded his police salary. He had school and other family stuff to pay for, but this...this was all too much for him to bear.

He'd had trouble sleeping and eating since that first time. Who knows what was happening to those kids? They could be dead for all he knew. Or worse. And then there was today. He'd seen a look in his partner's eyes today that he'd never seen before. Or maybe he'd just never paid attention to it until now. Either way, that look scared him. It was a needy, lustful look. Like how Slick always looked at women. Like how he imagined a hungry predator looked at its prey right before the kill.

He'd done a lot of dirt with Mayday over the years, and they had always come out on top with plenty of money in their hands to show for it. So, he never thought about questioning his partner or going against him in any way. But now, it was different. Maybe the money wasn't worth it after all. There were lines that should never be crossed, and Slick knew that they had crossed one of those lines. He also knew that he couldn't do this anymore, he wouldn't do it anymore. What would his family think of him if they knew what he was doing? What would happen to them if he and Mayday got caught?

He wanted out. There was no other way. He had to get out. But how? He had no idea how deeply they were involved in this thing. Had they gone too far to stop? Did Mayday even want to stop? And what would Slick do if he didn't?

PART TWO

"BEST FRIENDS"

CHAPTER 5

The Midwest – circa the mid-1990s…

Hakim was teasing him again. The two friends had been playing their game for most of the afternoon. They had a few games that they liked to play together. Today, they were playing their own special version of hide-and-seek. They had been playing for hours and they continued to play now, even as the sun eased towards the western edge of the cloudless sky, leaving orange and pink streaks across the pale blue backdrop.

The boy couldn't help but laugh at his friend as he watched Hakim hide again and again in the field. He made the tall, golden-green stalks shiver and wave as he dashed between the rows of corn. The two friends could've been mistaken for twins.

They were the same height and they shared the same shade of brown skin.

Each time the boy lost sight of Hakim, his friend would appear again moments later, poking his head from out of the thick crops of vegetation and making a silly face at the boy. He'd wave and the boy would wave back and then close his eyes and count to ten again. And when he opened them, Hakim would dart off again. The boy wished that their play time didn't have to end, but the day was almost gone now. He wouldn't be able to play with Hakim again until tomorrow, and only if he behaved and did as he was told.

The boy sat on the windowsill in his room, his small arms pulling his knees to his chin. He pressed his face to the window and could feel the chilled air when his nose touched the frosted glass. He laughed again when he saw Hakim dive into a pile of freshly raked leaves. His friend pretended to swim laps in the sea of foliage, kicking the red and orange leaves over his head. He watched with amazement as a gathering gust snatched up the leaves and made them drift slowly back to the ground. He wanted desperately to join his friend outside, but he knew that would never happen. So instead, he continued to watch his friend play until the nighttime shadows swallowed the last remnants of daylight. A chilly autumn day had turned into a freezing Nebraskan night. The boy hated the night because the nighttime was always the worst for him.

"Mikah!"

The boy heard her calling him from the front of the tiny apartment. Her voice sounded so far away, but she was just a few feet away in the next room. She was never that far from him when she was home, and she never let him get too far out of her sight. She usually called him when he'd been quiet for a while, just so she could know what he was doing.

"Mikah, you hear me calling you?" Her voice sounded hard and much closer as it pulled him from the playground in his mind. The boy knew Hakim had gone by now. He always left when she called, but Mikah waved towards the darkness anyway before climbing down from the window.

"Yes, Mommy?" Mikah answered knowing that if he didn't, she would come looking for him and that would not be good.

Janice wasn't his mommy, but she made him call her that, especially if they were around other people, which didn't happen a lot. She'd always made him call her mommy for as long as he could remember. She told him that she was his mommy, but he knew that wasn't the truth. Hakim had said so. His friend told him that many times when they talked late at night after Janice fell asleep.

Those late-night whispers with Hakim always helped him sleep better. Hakim also helped him not to cry as much when Janice punished him or made him stay by himself in the darkness. And he helped Mikah stay brave every time they went to a new place.

When Mikah had asked Janice why he had to call her "Mommy" when she wasn't his mommy, Janice had gotten mad. She'd screamed at him and grabbed his wrists so hard that he'd started crying. Janice told him that he had to call her Mommy or people would ask questions, and then he would get in trouble. He didn't want to get in trouble, did he? No, of course, he didn't. So, Mikah always called Janice "Mommy"; but he never forgot what his friend told him.

Mikah couldn't remember his mother anymore. He couldn't remember his father, either. Sometimes he tried hard to remember how his mommy looked. Tried to remember how his daddy looked, too. He tried so hard sometimes that he'd start to cry, frustrated at the lack of memories and vague, blurred pictures floating around in his head. He'd try and try, but their faces never came to him. His life before Janice never came to him, but he knew there had to be more. Hakim had told him there was more, and he believed his best and only friend.

Hakim had told him that he had parents and even a baby brother. *A baby brother?* Mikah had asked in amazement. Mikah wondered how he looked and what his name was. Hakim told him that his family missed him and would want to know where he was after all this time.

Mikah wondered where they were now, his mommy and daddy and the baby brother Hakim told him about. Were they still alive? Were they looking for him?

Hakim also told him that he'd been taken away from his family, but Mikah couldn't remember any of that either. Hakim told him about the men who'd taken him and how he came to live with Janice, but Mikah didn't want to believe that part was true. Why would someone want to take him from his parents and his brother? Didn't they know how much they would miss him? Why would anyone want to take any little kid from his family?

CHAPTER 6

"You smell that goodness, Mikah?" Janice called out to him, her voice sounding nicer now that he'd answered her. "Smells good, right? Come on, hurry up and come see what I cooked up."

Mikah left his room and walked down the narrow hallway towards the kitchen where Janice had been busy for the past few hours. They lived in a cramped one-bedroom apartment that was mostly empty. There was an inflatable bed in Mikah's room and a small blue plastic storage bin that held his few clothes and his single pair of sneakers when he wasn't wearing them. He also had a few books and several small toys, but not much else.

At the front of the apartment, there was a small, round wooden table with two worn plastic lawn chairs in the space just outside of the kitchen. A few feet away from the table sat a tattered, faded green couch and a small plastic and metal folding table. Janice usually ate her meals on the old couch so she could watch the small TV that sat on two red plastic crates stacked in a corner of the room. Janice also used that couch as her bed and usually fell asleep at night with the TV on.

Mikah sat in his usual place at the battered, shaky-legged table whose chipped white paint was almost all the way gone. With wide, hungry eyes he looked at the delicious-looking food spread out on the small table and the nearby counter.

There were dozens of cupcakes with pink, green, and yellow frosting. Mikah also saw two chocolate cakes and a few pies, but he couldn't tell what flavor the pies were. There was also a plate piled high with brownies. The mouth-watering aromas of the desserts wrapped themselves around Mikah and made his tummy growl. He hadn't eaten anything since the cheese sandwich and the cup of water he'd had for breakfast.

Janice stood at the stove with her back turned to him. She was wearing a light blue dress that fit tightly over her husky frame. Her strawberry blonde hair was pulled into a tight bun and Mikah could see the small, blue dolphin tattoo on the back of her pale, freckled neck. He started to reach for the plate of brownies sitting in the middle of the table, but of course, she saw him. She always saw him.

"Mm-mm, no, no, Mikah. Don't touch. Those are for the children at the church. You be a good boy and maybe I'll save you some."

He snatched his hand away and tucked it into his lap. Janice smiled and winked at Mikah. Her green eyes sparkled. She wore eye shadow and dark red lipstick, so Mikah knew she was going out tonight.

Janice was in a good mood right now, which was good for Mikah. But it wasn't always this way. When she was sad or angry, Janice was a much different person and that's when she scared Mikah the most.

"Did you finish your lessons?" Janice asked as she smoothed creamy icing on a batch of cupcakes she'd just pulled from the oven.

"Yes, ma'am," Mikah replied, his eyes locked on the cupcakes she was fussing over. "I finished them earlier today."

"Good boy," she replied. "I'll check them later."

"Mommy, how long are we staying in this place?" Mikah asked after he managed to tear his eyes away from the desserts. "I don't like it here."

Janice's smile vanished. She looked up from the cupcakes and gave him that look that usually meant he was in trouble. Realizing his mistake, Mikah's eyes grew wide with fear. He flinched and sunk lower into his chair. Mikah knew better than to ask such a stupid question. *Why did he always have to make Janice so mad? Stupid. So stupid.*

Mikah no longer cared about the desserts. He wanted to run and hide. Instead, he closed his eyes and held his breath, bracing for the slap, punch, kick, or belt-whipping he knew was coming.

"Sorry, Mommy," he said. "I'm sorry. I didn't mean to."

Janice fixed him with her hard stare for another few moments and then returned her attention to the cupcakes. Mikah let out a long sigh of relief. His heart was beating so fast that he felt dizzy.

"I already told you," she said. "As soon we pick up your new little brother or sister, we'll be on our way to our new home."

Hakim was standing beside Mikah's chair then, and he whispered in the boy's ear that they would move to another place that he didn't like. For the last two years, they had moved around a lot, going wherever Janice said they had to go, never staying in one place too long. Hakim told Mikah a lot of things that he couldn't possibly know. Most of all, he told Mikah the truth about Janice.

Mikah didn't want another brother or sister. He had Hakim. Besides, Janice always got angry with the new kids and sent them away. The last ones were Mikey and Michelle, the baby twins. They had lasted almost six months before they went away. Hakim said that Janice couldn't stand the constant crying.

There had also been Louis. He'd been tall and very skinny and very quiet, with red hair and freckles all over his face and arms. He was older than Mikah and had been there for as long as Mikah could remember. Louis never said much, and he always looked sad, but he'd been nice to Mikah. Then one day, Louis just didn't live with them anymore. Janice had taken him with her one morning and Mikah never saw him again. Louis was gone, and Mikah knew better than to ask about him.

He'd asked about the twins after they disappeared, and Janice had beat him something terrible and made him stay in the darkness for a week. She'd given him just a roll of Ritz crackers to eat and a large bottle of water to drink. He'd been forced to use a bucket as a toilet. After that, he knew better than to ever ask Janice about the other kids again.

Mikah often wondered why Janice never got rid of him like she had gotten rid of the others. *Where did those kids go? What had she done with them?* Hakim told him that bad things happened to them. When the new kids went away, the sadness always came around. Janice was sad for the next few days, and Mikah had to be sad too. Otherwise, Janice would get very mad at him. Mikah hated the sadness the same way he hated the darkness.

Tonight, Janice was going to a church social to find a new child to bring home. "Maybe even a brother *and* a sister," she said as she placed her freshly baked treats in Tupperware containers. Mikah watched Janice finish packing up the food and then grab her coat and scarf as she prepared to leave. She looked at him once over her shoulder, giving him that stare of hers that was as cold as a winter night.

Immediately, without a second thought, Mikah jumped out of his chair and started moving. He knew the drill now without her having to say a word. It was a fear-fueled reflex for him at this point.

He got up from the table and grabbed the cup of water, the napkin full of Goldfish crackers, and the two pills she'd sat out for him. His vitamins. That's what Janice always called them. *You have to take your vitamins, Mikah,* she would say, *so you won't get sick.* But the vitamins always made him sleepy, and sometimes they made his head foggy and his tummy ache.

He got up from the table and started to leave the kitchen, but Janice called after him. "Mikah," she said, "Did you forget something?"

"No, Mommy," he said, and he walked over and kissed her dryly on her cheek.

"What else?" she asked him.

Mikah placed the two pills in his mouth and took a sip of water.

"Good boy," Janice said and turned back to the stove. "Now, goodnight."

With his head down and without saying a word, he walked to the bathroom. He peed, washed and dried his hands and face, and then went into his room.

Mikah closed the bedroom door behind him, then walked across the room and opened the top of the plastic bin. He pulled out his lone pair of pajamas, a green and blue set that was faded, worn in the knees and the bottom, and too small for him now. He changed into the pajamas and placed the clothes and shoes he'd been wearing into the bin, then put the top back in place.

Mikah moved with a sense of urgency now, not wanting Janice to come in and check on him. It wouldn't be good if she did that. He grabbed the cup of water and napkin full of crackers and moved towards the small closet in the room. He opened the closet door, stepped inside and then closed the door behind him.

He sat cross-legged on the floor and called out, "I'm done, Mommy. Goodnight." She didn't respond, but he knew she was standing right outside of the bedroom door listening to his every move. After a while, he heard Janice leave the apartment, locking the door behind her.

CHAPTER 7

After a few minutes, when he was sure Janice was gone, Mikah put his hand below his mouth and spit the pills into his palm. Then he turned and crawled on his hands and knees towards the back of the closet. With his left hand, he reached out and tugged at a small piece of carpet in the floor. When the fabric came loose, he folded it back and dropped the pills into the space that held the others he'd placed there. Mikah pushed the fabric back down, then scooted back towards the front of the closet.

He'd been hiding his vitamins like this for a while now. Hakim had told him that the pills weren't vitamins at all and that he shouldn't take them anymore because they were bad for him.

At the front of the closet, Mikah reached out and found his cup of water and crackers. He'd spent so much time in the closet that he'd gotten pretty good at finding things in the dark without knocking them over. Janice made him go into the closet whenever she needed to leave their apartment. It had been this way wherever they went since Mikah had come to live with her all those months ago.

He lifted the cup to his lips and took a small sip. Then he carefully placed the cup back down on the floor, far enough away from his feet so he didn't accidentally knock it over. He took two of the twenty goldfish crackers, placed them in his mouth, and chewed slowly.

He'd learned the hard way that he needed to save his water and food because he never knew when Janice would come home. Sometimes it would be minutes, but most times it would be hours before she returned and let him out of the closet. If he drank all his water, he didn't know when he would get more and he would be thirsty. If he ate his food too soon, he would be starving by the time she let him out of the closet and allowed him to eat again.

Even worse, if Mikah drank all his water and peed himself or if he spilled the water and made a mess, Janice would find out and she would do something horrible to him. Maybe she would beat him or burn him with a hot hanger. Maybe both. She'd done these things to him before, and Mikah knew she'd do them again if he made her angry.

"Can't stay here, Mikah." He heard his friend's voice as he always did when they were alone. Hakim didn't talk as much when Janice was around, even though she couldn't see or hear him. Sometimes he whispered in Mikah's ear, but he mostly just stood nearby watching. There were also times when he didn't come around at all. That usually happened when Janice was doing something bad to Mikah.

"Can't stay here, Mikah. You can't stay here, man." Mikah heard Hakim whisper again when he didn't answer his friend.

"I can't leave," Mikah said in his own whisper, shaking his head from side-to-side. "Not supposed to leave this closet. Janice will be mad if I do. Remember what happened last time I went out there while she was gone?"

Hakim didn't answer, but Mikah knew he remembered what happened.

The last time Mikah left the closet while Janice wasn't home, it had turned into a bad night for him. Janice had gone out to shop or work or whatever it was she did when she left him alone.

He'd forgotten to use the bathroom before she left and after a few hours, he couldn't hold it anymore. Not wanting to pee himself because he knew what would happen if he did, he snuck out of the closet, used the bathroom and returned to the closet right after.

When Janice came home hours later, she'd immediately known what Mikah had done. He didn't know how, but she'd known. He thought maybe he left the toilet seat up or something like that. Mikah tried to explain, but Janice hadn't wanted to hear any of it.

She'd unleashed her fury upon him without hesitation. She beat him so badly that he couldn't sit down, sleep on his left side, or lift his left arm for almost a week. To make things worse, she also starved him during that entire week, not letting him have anything but a little bit of bread to eat and some warm water to drink. And she made him sleep in the closet...in the darkness.

Just the thought of it made Mikah's backside hurt and sent a wave of fear rushing through his body. A couple of tears filled his eyes, and he wiped at them with the back of his small, shaking hand. No, he couldn't leave this closet until Janice came home and let him out. Couldn't do it. He couldn't, and he wouldn't.

As if reading his mind, Hakim whispered again, *"Can't stay here, man. Have to leave away from here. Now."*

Mikah sniffled and exhaled a deep breath. He repeated the deep breathing, in and out, trying to calm himself down. Hakim taught him to do this so he wouldn't be too scared when he was in the dark.

"Why?" he asked. "Why do I have to leave? It's not so bad here. Plus, Janice said we would be leaving soon."

"Have to leave here, man," his friend whispered again. *"Have to. Tonight."*

"But why, Hakim?" Mikah said, feeling like he wanted to cry again. "Why do I need to leave now? And go where? I always sit in here every day, and I'm ok long as I don't break the rules, right?"

"If you don't leave tonight, Janice will hurt you again, but this time it will be really bad," his friend said. *"Worse than ever before."*

"No, Hakim," Mikah said, shaking his head from side to side. "Janice only hurts me if I'm bad, remember?"

"Maybe before, but not when she gets her new baby. Then she won't want you anymore."

Mikah grew quiet after hearing his friend's words. The darkness in the closet seemed to get a little darker then.

"Remember the others?" Hakim continued, his voice sounding far away. *"They went away, right?"*

"Yeah but..." Mikah said, still not wanting to believe his friend, "Nothing bad happened to them. They just went away. Went to live somewhere else, right? That's all."

"That's not true, Mikah," Hakim said. *"You know that's not what happened to those other kids."*

Mikah did know. Deep down, he knew the truth. Even at his young age, he knew all of this was wrong. He knew those other kids didn't go away to live somewhere else. He didn't want to believe it, but he knew that Janice had done something horrible to those other kids, just like she was going to do something horrible to Mikah one day.

But Janice wouldn't do that to *him*, would she? No, she wouldn't do that. She got angry and hurt him sometimes, but she wouldn't do *that* to him, right?

She said she loved Mikah. But, if she'd done that to the twins and to Louis, then why wouldn't she do it to him, too? Mikah had tried to be a good boy, to do what Janice wanted him to do, but maybe none of that would matter. Hakim had told him many times that she wasn't right in her head, that she was sick. Maybe his friend was right? Maybe Janice really was sick.

Mikah thought that when Janice returned later tonight, they would just pack up again and leave this place. Like they left when she'd come home with the twins or like the other times when Janice had said it was time for them to move again. They would start driving while it was still nighttime. Mikah would fall asleep and when he woke up, they would be in a new place. Another place that he wouldn't know and wouldn't like.

They had moved many times before, too many different places. Some of the places were hot, some were cold. In some places, it rained a lot and in others, not much at all. Sometimes there was a lot of snow, and sometimes there was hardly any or none at all. Mikah was always scared to move to a new place, but he didn't worry about it as much anymore. Not since Hakim had come into his life.

His friend had shown up right after one of their moves, and since then he traveled with them everywhere they went. So long as he was around, Mikah knew everything would be ok.

Hakim whispered to him again that they had to do something, that he had to get away from Janice tonight. His friend reminded him of the milk cartons. The ones with the pictures of missing little kids like him and the words that said how to help those kids. As Mikah sat there in the dark thinking of what he could possibly do, Hakim reminded him of the telephone. *A telephone.* Janice had a telephone that they could use to call for help.

Mikah knew that Janice kept it hidden away unless she was using it, which didn't happen a lot. Once, she'd been using the phone and saw Mikah looking at it after she finished her call. She'd pinched his ear so hard that he thought she might rip it off.

"Don't you ever even think about touching it, you hear?" she'd screamed at him. Mikah had promised that he wouldn't touch it as he cried and begged her to stop hurting him. But now, he needed to break that promise.

Hakim told Mikah where Janice kept the phone. All Mikah had to do now was get it and call someone. Mikah eased open the closet door and stepped out of the darkness. He took a few timid steps towards Janice's bags and felt the familiar ache of fear in his legs, arms, and hands as he began to shake all over. He couldn't do this. He just couldn't.

"I-I can't," he said as he started to turn back towards the closet, his voice unable to rise above a frightened whisper. "Janice will know."

"But you have to, Mikah," Hakim said in his ear again, all his usual playfulness long gone. *"You have to or more kids will get hurt just like you. Just like the other kids that used to live with you and Janice."*

Mikah didn't want other kids to end up trapped like him, never knowing where he was or where he would end up. Unable to do anything but what Janice told him. Living in constant fear. Experiencing the kind of pain that no child should ever have to endure. Mikah didn't want to live that way anymore.

He couldn't remember exactly where he was from, but he knew enough to know that he didn't belong here with Janice. He also knew that she wasn't a good person, and he couldn't let her hurt any more kids like she'd hurt him. Most of all, he couldn't let any more kids end up like Louis and the twins.

CHAPTER 8

Janice had three bags that she always took with them whenever they moved. One was a worn green backpack, the second was a larger blue duffle bag that was just as worn as the backpack, and the last one was a black rolling suitcase.

"The suitcase," Hakim told Mikah. *"In the front pocket. The phone is in there."*

"How do you know?" Mikah asked his friend.

"Because we've seen her put it in there before. Look in there."

Mikah didn't remember seeing anything like that, but he listened to his friend and unzipped the front pocket of the black suitcase. He started to reach his hand inside, but Hakim called out to him.

"Wait, Mikah," Hakim told him. *"Unzip it all the way first, and don't reach inside."*

Mikah did as he was told and tugged on the zipper until it moved from one side of the bag to the other. The suitcase's front pocket flap folded over onto itself allowing the pocket's contents to spill out. He heard two loud snaps as everything inside the pocket fell onto the carpeted floor.

He saw the cordless phone. But he also saw the cause of the snapping sounds and the reason Hakim had stopped him from reaching inside. Two large mousetraps had been set and placed in the pocket with the phone. They would've broken Mikah's small fingers if he'd reached inside.

"Thanks," Mikah told his friend. He picked up the cordless phone, removing it from its cradle, which Mikah could now see was plugged into nearby electrical and phone outlets. The outlets and the phone's cords had been hidden by the suitcase. Although the mousetraps had been triggered, Mikah was careful to avoid touching them.

He pushed the phone's power button. It came on and the phone's numbers lit up in a bright green. He could hear the dial tone. Hakim told Mikah to dial 9-1-1, and Mikah pressed the numeric buttons and then the button with the green phone symbol.

Mikah put the phone to his ear and heard the other line ring once before a woman's voice said, "9-1-1, what is your emergency?"

Mikah didn't know what to say, so he stayed silent.

"Hello," the woman said, sounding almost like a robot. "9-1-1, what is your emergency?"

Mikah heard Hakim whispering in his ear, encouraging him to speak up and he said, "H-hello?"

"Yes? Hello?" the woman said, irritation creeping into her tone. "Young man, this line is for emergencies. Do you have an emergency?"

"I-I need help," Mikah said, finding his courage. "Please come and get me. Please...she, she's gonna hurt me. Please help me."

"Who's going to hurt you?" the woman said, concern replacing the earlier irritation in her voice. "Are you ok? What's your name?"

"J-Janice," Mikah said trying to cling to his fleeting courage, his words coming out in a stutter.

"Janice?" the woman on the other end said. "Your name is Janice?"

"N-no, ma'am. Janice makes me stay here in the darkness. I need help. M-my name is...my name is…Janice told me to tell everyone that my name is Mikah. P-Please, help me."

The woman asked him where he was, but Mikah had no clue.

"I-I don't know," he told her, frustration and fear working hard on him now. He felt the hot tears returning to his eyes. "I don't know where I am. But I'm scared. I'm not supposed to be using Janice's phone, not supposed to mess with Janice's things."

The emergency dispatcher told Mikah to look out of a window and tell her what he saw. Mikah did as he was told. He was able to describe a couple of nearby houses, a street sign, and a large red and white water tower near the railroad tracks.

The woman told him not to hang up the phone, but Mikah told her that Janice would be home soon and that he had to get back in the darkness before she came back. The woman on the phone told him he had to stay on the phone so she could find him. She said she would send help to him, but he had to stay on the phone. Mikah promised not to hang up, telling the woman that he would try to stay on the line for as long as he could.

CHAPTER 9

Mikah was still holding the phone in his hand when he heard the front door of the apartment unlock and begin to open. He was standing in the middle of the bedroom and heard Janice's voice calling out to him as she came through the door.

He knew he should run, put the phone back, and get back in the closet. But he couldn't move. Fear had frozen his feet in place.

"Mikah," she called in the sing-song voice she used when she was in a good mood. "Come on out of that closet now, sweetheart. I've got a surprise for you."

"You hear me, Mikah?" she called again. "Come meet your new baby brother. He's just as precious as..."

Janice's words trailed off when she looked down the hallway and saw Mikah standing in the middle of the bedroom holding her phone.

"Mikah," she said in what sounded more like a growl than actual words, "What... are... you... doing? And what the hell are you doing with that phone?"

Her eyes grew big and feral, and she took two slow steps in his direction. Without taking her eyes off him, Janice placed the bundle she was carrying on the couch.

"Mikah," she yelled. "Come here...*right now*!"

Out of reflex and as if in a trance, Mikah began walking towards Janice.

"Don't," Mikah heard Hakim say in his ear. *"Don't do it. Lock the door. LOCK THE DOOR, MIKAH!"*

He jumped at his friend's words and ran towards the bedroom door. Janice's steps boomed in the small hallway as she stomped towards the bedroom. Mikah managed to shut the door and lock it just as she reached it. She pounded hard on the door and jiggled the lock as she screamed for him to open the door. Mikah heard the sound of a baby starting to cry. He squeezed the phone in his hand and raised it to his ear.

"H-Hello," he whispered into the phone. "Are you coming to get me? Janice is home. *Please*, you said you were coming to get me."

The dispatcher's voice cracked with fear when she told him, "Just hold on, baby. Help is almost there. It's almost there. Almost. Do you have a place where you can hide?"

Janice continued to bang on the door and scream for him to open it. Her screams grew louder, and she started kicking the door. He heard the door's lock rattle as it began to buckle beneath her assault. Mikah began backing up towards the closet. The door groaned and pushed inward. He heard a metal popping sound as the lock gave way, and the door flew inward, smashing into the bedroom wall.

Janice rushed into the room and moved her head from side to side, trying to see exactly what he'd been doing. She looked down at the open pocket of her suitcase and the mousetraps on the floor.

"Where is it?" she said turning her attention to Mikah. Too scared to do anything else, he'd moved to the other side of the room and had tried to tuck himself into a corner behind his air mattress.

"Where is it? Where is my phone, you little sonofabitch? *Where is it??* You give me that damn phone right now or else!"

He hid the phone behind his back as Janice stepped on the air mattress and closed the space between them. He pushed himself back into the corner as far as he could go.

"Give me that phone, Mikah, damn it! Give it to me now!" She stood in front of Mikah, towering over him as she reached for him.

"NO!" he yelled back at Janice, "Don't touch me!"

Mikah heard the words as they came out of his mouth, but the voice did not sound like his own. Instead, he heard Hakim's voice as if his friend was speaking for him. But these were his words, and this was his voice.

His rebuke momentarily shocked Janice, causing her to pull back her arm. But then she grabbed his right arm tightly and twisted it, trying to force it from behind his back. Mikah cried out and pulled away from her grip. He kicked Janice hard in the shin and she doubled over in pain, cursing as she reached for her injured leg.

He ran towards the bedroom door, but Janice managed to grab him from behind. Tugging hard at the back of his shirt, she snatched him off of his feet and threw him backward. His body crashed into the wall and then crumpled to the floor. But he managed to hold onto the phone. Pain seized Mikah's body. He felt dizzy and his eyesight grew blurry.

Get up, he heard Hakim's voice in his head, *get up, Mikah.* He pushed himself up, but before he could stand, Janice was on top of him. She pulled him up by the front of his shirt and slapped him hard across his face and then gut-punched him. She shoved him back into the wall and then yanked him forward again. Then she picked him up and slammed him back onto the hard floor. He felt the phone fly out of his hand. He tasted blood and felt like he would vomit. His head and stomach hurt bad, and the edges of his vision began to go dark.

Janice punched him again, this time in his face, and he bit his tongue when the back of his head smacked against the floor. He could no longer suppress his nausea and the hot bile burned his throat as he turned his head to the side and vomited the remains of his last meal onto the floor.

He felt her hands around his throat, and she began to squeeze. Mikah clawed at her hands, scratching and pulling at her fingers as he tried to twist out of her grip. But she held tight like a pit bull locked onto someone's arm. Janice squeezed his neck tighter and shook him, hitting the back of his head on the floor.

She screamed at him through gritted teeth, spit flying from her mouth and landing on his face as she said, "I loved you like my own child. Why couldn't you just listen and do what you were told? Why must you be a bad child, Mikah? Why? Why? Why?"

Mikah gasped and tried to speak, but Janice tightened her grip. She was going to kill him. He was going to die. He saw Hakim standing in the corner, tears rolling down his cheeks. Hakim swung his fists wildly through the air like he was trying to hit Janice, but of course, he couldn't hit her. He was helpless and couldn't do anything but sit and watch as she murdered his friend. The help the lady on the phone had promised wasn't coming. Mikah shut his eyes and felt his own grip loosening on Janice's hands as he gasped the last of his remaining breaths.

Then Mikah heard a loud banging at the front door. He thought maybe he was imagining it, but then he heard it again. He opened his eyes. Janice was still on top of him, holding him down. Her hands were still around his throat, but her grip had relaxed. Mikah could still hear the baby's cries, but he also heard someone yelling from behind the front door. He couldn't be sure, but he thought he heard them yelling, "Police!"

Janice had heard it, too, and she released her hold on Mikah and lifted herself off of him. He gasped and coughed and felt a sharp pain in his throat and chest as fresh air rushed into his lungs. Through watery eyes, Mikah saw Janice run over to her bags and reach into the green backpack. When her hand reappeared, it held a small gun. Janice looked at him and raised the gun, pointing it at him. Mikah sat there on the floor, unable to move. Then, Janice's face transformed from a mask of anger and hatred into one of sadness as tears spilled from her eyes and ran down her reddened cheeks.

"I loved you. You were my baby boy," she said. Then she lowered the weapon, turned away from Mikah, and walked towards the front of the apartment.

Mikah remained motionless until a large crashing sound shook him out of his trance. He jumped up from the floor, ran into the closet and closed the door behind him. He pushed himself as far to the back of the closet as possible and sat down on the floor. Mikah covered his ears with his hands, tucked his head down, and hugged his knees to his chest. Yells and a loud bang that sounded like a gunshot came from the front of the apartment. Then he heard more yells, followed by more loud noises that sounded like footsteps and things being knocked over. And then, he didn't hear anything.

After a few minutes, the closet door opened and Mikah heard a voice calling out to him.

"Mikah? Mikah, you in here? It's ok. Come on out. It's ok. She won't hurt you anymore."

Mikah looked up and saw a young white woman in a police uniform reaching out to him. She smiled at him. She had friendly brown eyes and dark brown hair and looked nothing like Janice. Mikah hesitated, but then he took the woman's outstretched hand and allowed himself to be led out of the closet. As he followed the policewoman towards the front of the apartment, he saw Janice's body lying on the floor. A blanket covered most of her body, but he could see the bottoms of her legs and shoes. Splotches of dark crimson stained the blanket.

He also saw a policeman holding the baby Janice had brought home. The baby continued to cry even as the policeman rocked it side to side, trying to soothe it.

Mikah heard a couple of the other officers talking about Janice and how she'd taken her own life to avoid being arrested. The officers also talked about how she'd been suspected in the abduction of several other kids. Apparently, Janice moved from town to town, worked a few odd jobs, and then disappeared again before anyone could catch up to her.

Mikah remembered now. Everything Hakim had always told him was true. And he remembered all of it now. He remembered the men who had taken him. How they kept him locked in a dark room, bringing him a little bit of food and something to drink once a day. How they gave him a bucket to use as a bathroom and another bucket of water, a bar of soap, and a towel to wash up.

He also remembered the terrible things one of the men had done to him. He remembered how the man had hurt him. How he touched him and did other things to him, and how the man forced Mikah to do bad things to him. He remembered how the man beat him. And how he threatened to kill him if he ever told anyone. He didn't know the man's name, but he remembered the man's face, his voice, and his smell. He remembered hearing the men talk about how much money they would get for him. All of it. He remembered every horrible detail of his few days with those men before they had taken him to another man. This was the man who had brought him to Janice.

After a medic treated Mikah's injuries, the same policewoman led him outside to a waiting car. As he walked down the sidewalk, Mikah looked back over his shoulder towards the apartment. Hakim appeared in the same window where Mikah had spent so many hours staring outside watching his friend play. He'd always wondered what it would be like to go outside and play with him. Now he was the one outside and Hakim was the one staring at him from the window. His friend waved to him from the window and Mikah waved back. Then Hakim stepped back from the window and slowly disappeared from view.

Mikah's best friend, though just a figment of his imagination, had helped him get away from Janice, and he knew that Hakim would be there if he ever needed him again. Because that's what best friends did for each other.

"You know, it isn't your fault what happened in there," the policewoman said as they walked down the steps, "You know that, right? Janice Reynolds was a very bad, very sick person."

"Yeah, I know," Mikah said without looking up at her.

"What's your name, honey? I mean, your real name?"

Mikah stopped walking and looked up at the policewoman, unsure of how to answer her question. Then he shook his head and looked away from her. He used the back of his hand to wipe away the tears. He was tired of crying.

"It's ok, honey. You can tell me," the policewoman coaxed. "She changed your name, right? Made you call yourself Mikah? That's what you told the operator on the phone?"

Mikah looked up at the policewoman again, his lips trembled as he answered,

"Y-yeah, she called me Mikah and made me call her mommy."

The policewoman kneeled in front of Mikah and said, "Janice used to have a son named Mikah, but he died in an accident when he was just a baby. We know that Mikah isn't your name. So, why don't you tell me your name so we can get you back to your family? You would like that right?"

Mikah nodded. He did want to go home. *His* home, to be with *his* family. He wanted that more than anything in the world.

"My name is Reggie," he said, "but my parents and my brother used to call me Beanie."

PART THREE

“BROKEN FOREVER”

CHAPTER 10

In the two years that went by after Beanie was taken, his parents never stopped searching for their missing son. They posted flyers, knocked on doors, organized more search parties, and contacted news outlets. They hounded the police relentlessly. But, still, there hadn't been any news. Beanie was simply gone.

But Scoop never forgot about his big brother. He stayed out of Beanie's room, never once touching his things, not even his Nintendo. That's what Beanie would want, so that's what he did. He held on tight to the idea that he would see his brother again, refusing to believe that Beanie was gone forever.

Sometimes, late at night, after his parents had gone to sleep, Scoop lay awake thinking of his brother and that terrible day. He'd end up crying himself to sleep but would wake up a few hours later yelling for his parents after having a nightmare. The images of Beanie and the men who took him haunted Scoop. On those nights, he'd end up sleeping in his parents' bed, unable to get back to sleep in his own.

He often bombarded his parents with questions about Beanie's whereabouts. Questions they couldn't answer. Day after day went by, but nothing seemed to matter to them anymore. His parents stopped talking as much. Sometimes they would argue. Other times they just sat in their room holding one another and crying together. Scoop could hear them through the apartment's thin walls, and sometimes he'd peek in on them when they hadn't remembered to close their door. The sounds of his mother's long, anguished moans and sobbing also plagued Scoop's dreams. He wanted it all to stop.

In the midst of his parents' misery, Scoop just kind of disappeared from their view and seemed to fold in on himself. His parents continued to do the basic providing for him of course, but that was it. In those two years, Scoop learned to rely on himself more than anyone else. Things for their family had changed to the point where he thought he would never know normal again.

And then one day, just like that, everything changed again for Scoop and his family. After two years of almost no useful information from the police or anyone else, Scoop's parents received a shocking phone call as the family was sitting down to dinner. He had no way of knowing who was on the other end, but he heard his parents' shouts and cries of joy at the news they had just received. *Beanie had been found...and he was alive!*

The next evening, the police brought Beanie back home. Scoop had been waiting in his room, not wanting to get his hopes up too much in case the police had made some terrible mistake. But they hadn't made a mistake. They kept their promise. He heard the commotion when his brother arrived and, not sure what else to do, he crept to the edge of the hallway to try and eavesdrop.

When Scoop saw Beanie for the first time, his brother looked different to him. He recognized Beanie, but he'd changed in the two years he'd been gone. He was taller and a whole lot skinnier. One of his eyes was swollen, his face and neck were bruised, and his bottom lip was split and puffy. He walked with a slight limp and his expression was a blank one, even as their parents wrapped him in hugs and showered him with kisses.

Their parents followed those hugs and kisses with desperate questions to Beanie about what happened to him. Scoop never heard what Beanie told their parents. They sent him to his room while they talked to his brother, which was ok with Scoop. He didn't want to know what those men had done to Beanie, where they had taken him. He was just happy that his brother was back home.

CHAPTER 11

In the days after he came home, his brother had seemed ok. Almost normal. But even at just nine years old, Scoop could tell that his older brother was anything but ok and not even close to normal.

More than Beanie's physical appearance had changed. He was damaged on the inside. He reminded Scoop of a broken toy that someone had Krazy-Glue'd back together. Sure, it worked and looked ok, but it was never quite right. That was his brother now. Put back together and not quite right.

Even after his physical wounds healed, the mental ones lingered. Beanie didn't laugh and play with Scoop like he used to before everything happened. He no longer hung out with friends, and he didn't show much interest in school. He even gave Scoop his Nintendo. As the days, months, and years went by, Beanie became someone that Scoop no longer knew.

Beanie tried his best to be normal again, but he just wasn't able to manage it. And Scoop and their parents were powerless to stop Beanie's mental and physical deterioration. They all tried to reach him in their own way. Scoop tried to get Beanie to hang out and play with him. Their parents tried talking to Beanie and getting him involved in the things he used to enjoy, like sports. When that didn't work, they almost bankrupted themselves sending Beanie to therapy sessions with several different doctors. None of it helped.

Scoop remembered overhearing his parents discussing what one doctor had told them: that someone with Beanie's level of PTSD may never make it all the way back. Even after he looked up the definition, Scoop wasn't sure exactly what PTSD meant, but he knew it wasn't good. He saw firsthand the effects of the abuse Beane had suffered.

CHAPTER 12

Beanie had returned home, and everything should've gone back to normal. But it hadn't and Scoop knew that life for his family would never be normal again. Their parents tried their best to get their lives back on track and as close to normal as possible. The boys were older now, but after what happened, their mom took a new job that allowed her to be home more often. She drove the boys to school each day and picked them up in the afternoon. Scoop wanted to complain to his mom about them being treated like babies, but he knew why she was doing it. After what happened to his brother, Scoop knew better than to question his mother's over-protective nature.

One afternoon, after Beanie had been home for a few months, the two brothers were with their mother at a grocery store not far from their home.

Their mom sent the boys into the store to pick up a few items while she waited in the car.

"What you think, Beanie?" Scoop said holding up two boxes of cereal, "Cocoa Puffs or Frosted Flakes?"

"Don't matter, man," Beanie mumbled. "Whatever you want. I'll eat either one." He was holding a box of Wheaties that had a picture of Michael Jordan on the front.

"Come on, man," Scoop said, "I can't decide. Help me choose, bro."

"Nah, you pick, Scoop," Beanie said. "You like cereal more than -... "

Beanie's words trailed off before he finished his sentence.

"What you say, bro?" Scoop asked as he continued to study the boxes of cereal.

When Beanie didn't reply, Scoop looked up and saw that his brother was no longer standing beside him. Instead, he'd turned his back to Scoop and had begun walking towards the front of the aisle.

"Yo!" Scoop called after his brother as he placed both boxes of cereal in their grocery cart. "Where you going, man?" He remembered their mother's order for him to stay with Beanie at all times and he hurriedly pushed the cart after his brother.

Beanie took hurried steps as he turned the corner at the front of the aisle. He dropped the box of cereal he'd been holding, and Scoop picked it up and placed it back on the shelf as he followed behind his brother.

Beanie walked to the end of the next aisle and then froze in his tracks. Scoop left the cart behind and jogged to catch up with his older brother.

"What's up with that, man?" Scoop said as he came up behind his brother. "Why you walk off like that?"

Beanie didn't answer, so Scoop stepped around him and looked up at his brother. Beanie wore an expression that Scoop had never seen before. His eyes were wide with fear and his mouth hung open. Tears had formed in the rims of Beanie's eyes. Scoop looked down and saw that his brother's hands had formed into tight fists that were pounding against the sides of his legs.

"Beanie, what's up, man? Why you look like that? You good bro?" Scoop said as he followed his brother's line of sight, trying to see exactly what his brother was staring at.

From what Scoop could tell, Beanie was staring at a man standing in front of the frozen meat section. The man's back was to them, but Scoop could see he was a large, white dude.

Scoop turned back to his brother and said, "Beanie, what the hell, man? What you looking at?"

"T-that's..." Beanie struggled to say, but he couldn't quite get his words out. "That's...that's..."

"That's who?" Scoop asked, but then it occurred to him exactly who his brother was looking at. Who else could it be? And just like that, Scoop was transported back to that horrible day when Beanie had been snatched from their lives.

"That's one of them, bro? It's one of them, isn't it?"

Beanie turned then and looked at Scoop, the tears that had formed in his eyes fell now, forming streaks down both of his cheeks. The look of pain and fear on Beanie's face scared Scoop. He looked down and saw that a dark wet spot had formed on the front of Beanie's jeans.

Scoop looked around and found a nearby restroom. He grabbed his brother's shirt sleeve and pulled him towards it. As they moved towards the restroom, he looked over his shoulder and saw that the man was still standing in the same spot with his back to them.

Scoop led his brother, who was almost catatonic at this point, into the first stall after they entered the bathroom.

He got his brother to sit down on the toilet and stepped out of the stall closing the door behind him. He went to the sink and pulled several paper towels from the nearby dispenser. He placed the towels under the faucet, turned the water on, and allowed the cool water to completely soak the paper towels. He placed one of the towels under the soap dispenser and pushed the handle until a good amount of foamy soap fell onto the wet paper towel. Scoop turned the water off and went back into the stall. He placed the soapy towel in Beanie's lap and used the others to wipe his brother's face. Beanie blinked as the cool water seemed to bring him back around.

He looked at Scoop and said, "That man, the one by the meats, he..."

"I know, bro," Scoop said, cutting him off. "I know, man. Stay here and use these towels to clean yourself up. I'll be right back, ok? Just stay here."

Beanie didn't answer. Instead, he picked up the towels and began wiping at the front of his pants.

Scoop stood there for a second looking at his older brother and felt an overwhelming sadness for his childhood idol. He exited the stall, closing the door behind him. Scoop walked out of the bathroom and headed directly for the frozen meats section. When he reached the section, the man was no longer standing there.

No!

Scoop looked up and down several aisles but did not see the man.

He can't be gone, Scoop thought to himself.

Scoop began frantically looking around the store, fearing that the man had left. Then, as he jogged to the rear of the store, he saw the man standing near the vegetable section. Scoop moved towards a nearby stack of tomatoes just a few feet from where the man was standing. The man was holding a couple of heads of lettuce and appeared to be trying to decide between the two.

Scoop tried to get a good look at the man's face without staring, but the man noticed Scoop looking at him.

"Help you, son?" the man said without looking at Scoop.

Scoop looked into his face and saw the same face he remembered from that horrible day.

"Uh," Scoop said, trying to think of something to say, "Sorry, I, uh, thought I knew you. My bad."

The man placed the two heads of lettuce back in their place and turned to face Scoop. He looked Scoop up and down and a wide grin crossed his face.

"Oh, yeah?" the man said. "Who are you looking for?"

"Um, not looking for anyone, but you kinda looked like my gym teacher, that's all."

The man laughed and stepped closer to Scoop.

"Son, I ain't nobody's gym teacher. But you look familiar to me, too. I know you?"

Scoop felt like he'd made a mistake. Maybe the man would remember him from that day as well. The back of his neck and the palms of his hands grew hot and slick with sweat.

"Don't think so," Scoop said and looked down at his feet.

"Where you from, son? You stay around here? What's your name?"

Scoop wanted to lie, but he couldn't think of anything to say that he thought sounded believable.

"Not far from here," Scoop said. "From the neighborhood. Everybody calls me Scoop."

"Hmm. Alright, Scoop," the man said, his eyes studying Scoop more closely now. "Maybe that's how I know you. I'm police. I patrol around here from time to time."

"Police?" Scoop said and took a step backward.

"Don't fret, son," the man said and gave Scoop a reassuring smile. "I ain't that kind of police. Unless you dealin' drugs, I ain't interested in you. You don't deal do you?"

"No sir," Scoop said. "I just go to school is all."

"Well, good," the man said. "Too many dealers around here as is."

The man reached into the front pocket of his jeans and pulled out a small white card. He handed the card to Scoop.

"My name is Detective Jacobs. You see or hear anything having to do with drugs, you let me know, you hear?"

Scoop took the card, looked at it and said, "Yes sir."

"Alright now, you be good, little man. And stay in school, hear?"

"Yes sir," Scoop said again.

"See you around, lil' man."

The man grabbed a head of lettuce, tossed it in his cart, and steered it away from Scoop towards the front of the store.

Scoop looked down at the card he held in his hand. It read: *Detective Mark Jacobs.*

He placed the card in his front pants pocket. Then he turned and headed back towards the bathroom to get his brother.

I'll see you around, Detective.

CHAPTER 13

Late one night, not too long after the grocery store incident, a sound that could best be described as a dying animal pulled Scoop from his sleep. When he sat up in his bed, he didn't hear anything and thought maybe the noise had been part of his dreams. Then he heard it again. Muffled sobs and moans. He crept out of his bed and followed the sound out of his room and across the hallway to Beanie's room. Slowly, Scoop eased the door open, stepped inside of the dark room, and closed the door behind him.

"Beanie, you in here, bro?" he whispered. "You alright?"

Yellow light from a streetlamp shone through the bedroom's window and allowed Scoop to see that Beanie wasn't in his bed. Scoop looked around the room and followed the sounds to the closet. The door of the closet was open, and he could see that

Beanie was sitting inside, cross-legged on the floor. His head was buried in his hands and his body shook as he sobbed. Scoop knelt down and when he reached out and touched his brother's shoulder, Beanie flinched as if he'd been slapped.

Scoop didn't say a word. Instead, he squeezed into the closet and wrapped his arms around his older brother, pulling him in close. Beanie crumbled into him and, not knowing what else to do, Scoop began rocking back and forth trying to comfort his brother as he continued to sob and shake uncontrollably.

"It's ok, Big Bro," Scoop said after a few minutes. "It's alright, man. I got you. It's gonna be ok now."

The two brothers remained there in that closet for the rest of the night until the sun rose the next morning.

Things got worse for Beanie after that night. He eventually dropped out of school and, in-between several stints in "juvie," he became addicted to drugs and alcohol. Scoop couldn't imagine the hell that Beanie had been forced to endure while he was gone, so he couldn't blame him for his addictions.

Whatever happened to him during the two years after he'd been taken changed and broke Beanie. It had changed and broken everything in their world. Forever.

PART FOUR

"SKELETONS AND DEMONS"

CHAPTER 14

Washington, D.C. – present day...

Metropolitan Police Department patrolman Fred Mooney was tired as hell. And not just regular ol' tired. No sir. Tonight, he had that deep, all in your muscles and bones, sleep for days, dog-ass tired working on him. Like an old-ass, broke-dick hound, that's exactly how he was feeling right about now. Hell, this was how he'd been feeling for a long while now.

He'd almost finished his thermos of tepid, stale coffee, but the caffeine hadn't helped him a damn bit. His feet and knees ached with a steady throbbing as he shifted his weight from one hurting foot to the other.

Damn dogs are barking loud tonight, he thought to himself.

He'd given up sitting in the car a while ago after his ass cheeks lost all feeling and he'd begun to doze off. For the last hour or so, Fred had resorted to leaning on the hood of his MPD cruiser.

To make matters worse, the weather was going to shit. Fat drops of rain fell from the nighttime sky, and a stiff wind forced Fred to turn up the collar on his uniform jacket. He'd finished up the last of his water and snacks almost an hour and a half ago and now his stomach was growling like a rabid dog. *Well hell, that was ok,* he reasoned. He needed to drop a few pounds anyway. More than a few, truth be told.

Over the last year or so, Fred had eaten more fast food than anyone should, and his waistline had paid the price. Damn Mickey D's, KFC, and Popeyes will get you every time.

He knew his constant aches and pains were a direct result of the extra weight he was carrying. And he didn't even want to know about his current cholesterol levels. His bad cholesterol was probably sky high. Last thing he needed in his life was a damn heart attack. But maybe a heart attack would put him out of his misery and rescue him from the hell he was currently living in.

Fred's shift had ended almost an hour ago, but as usual, his relief was late. It was the third time this week and at least the eighth or ninth time this month. He was a team player and all, but he'd had enough of this shit. As much as he hated to admit it, Fred knew it was time to run this mess on up the chain.

He wasn't no snitch, but he would have to speak to his shift supervisor on this one. Otherwise, it would get worse. Fred knew this to be the truth. These things always got worse if you didn't nip them in the bud early on.

Newbie patrolman Stevie Riley was scheduled to relieve Fred, but the kid was about as reliable as a pair of holey shoes in a rainstorm. The youngster had been on the force for a few months, while Fred had spent most of his adult life as a member of the Metropolitan Police Department. Fred had been born and raised in D.C. and had joined the force at age twenty-one after three years in the Navy.

Now, here he was almost forty years later. He was on his way out the damn door, but this kid had just gotten in the game. Fred remembered what that was like in the beginning, just starting out, being given a shit detail to earn your stripes. He knew how the kid felt. Ambition and boredom were a bad mix, especially for a cop. But this Riley kid was undependable and green, and he needed to get his shit together.

Maybe Fred would talk to him one more time before running it up to the bosses. He'd tried before, but the kid had ignored his "old school, grandpa talk."

The kid said Fred just didn't understand what it was like these days.

"Yeah, I hear you, Pops," Riley had told him during their last talk as he played with his cell phone. Looking at that idiotic Facebook foolishness. Killing off his damn brain cells. That's what was wrong with his generation anyway.

Fred didn't want to run this up the chain. A blemish on the rookie's record could hurt him long-term, but the kid clearly wasn't ready for primetime. He could use a strong dose of tough love. Maybe that would scare him straight.

For Fred, this slow-crawling mid-shift detail had been a welcomed distraction. A good way to get out of the house and keep on working one of the few jobs he'd ever known. His crime-fighting days on the street chasing down bad guys and closing cases were long behind him. And he couldn't stomach being a damn meter maid, writing tickets and shit like that. Hell no, better to stand a post in the middle of the night with no one around to see his shame. So here he was, in the cold and alone, waiting for this idiot to come to work so he could go home and be alone some more. But at least then he would be dry and warm.

Everything had changed for Fred after he'd lost his wife, Meggy, to cancer. He'd been set to retire almost two years ago. But when his beloved passed, he traded in the suit and his detective's badge and went back to patrol just to keep on living. His world had crumbled when Meggy succumbed to her disease, and the job was all he had to try and beat back the loneliness and heartbreak. Hell, for a while he'd needed the job just to have a reason to keep on waking up every day. Maybe he still did.

This patrol assignment at an industrial park on the Northeast side of the city had been a favor from up on high. He and the chief had been classmates at the academy and when Fred's life fell apart, the chief had looked out for him. One minute, he'd been ready to close the book on his career and the next, a doctor was delivering Meggy's death sentence.

They were supposed to spend their golden years traveling, spoiling their grandkids, and just enjoying the hell out of life. That was the plan. And then it all went to shit. The eighteen months that Meggy had spent battling her illness had been gut-wrenching. It had been pure torture for Fred to watch the love of his life just waste away while he stood by unable to do a damn thing to stop it. Her passing had almost been a mercy for the both of them.

All favors ran out eventually. Fred knew this to be an undeniable fact. Life moved on with or without you, didn't much matter if you wanted it to or not. Time just kept on ticking and the sand kept on running out of that hourglass. He'd been sitting still for too long, and soon enough he would need to move on with the business of living before his time ran out for good. But what was he supposed to do now that forced retirement was staring him in the face?

The department needed to free up slots for the new recruits, and Fred was burned out anyway. He was tired and his ass was dragging bad. He wasn't that old in years, but he had a lot of wear and tear on him. Both mental and physical. He'd lived hard, fast, and mostly wrong, and it had definitely done a number on him. They say age ain't nothing but a number. Well, Fred felt like his number was closer to a hundred instead of closer to sixty.

Deep-set lines creased his cheeks and forehead and heavy bags crowded the space beneath his eyes. Eyes that no longer held a spark and instead sported that glazed-over, faraway look. The whites of those eyes were no longer white. They were more like a pale, sickly yellowish color. A result of hitting the bottle too much over the years. His dark skin had long lost its glow and looked dull and weathered. His hair, cut close to his scalp these days, had all gone to gray. Shoulders that were once broad and strong now slumped under the weight of life. Thirty-five years of marriage. Gone. Almost forty as police. Soon to be gone. So, what was left for a used up, washed up cop like him?

His two kids, Sherry and Jeff, were grown and had lives and families of their own. The job had robbed them of their dad and his time too often while they were growing up. Missed birthdays, science fairs, graduations, sporting events, recitals, and on and on. All for the job. These days, he and his kids were more like strangers who happened to share the same blood.

He'd hoped retirement would give him the chance to reconnect with his kids and get to know his grandkids. But after Meggy died, the distance between him and the kids seemed to grow. He figured the kids blamed him for the way their mother had died. He hadn't been much of a husband or a father, and all he had left at this point were "maybes." Maybe if he'd been around more often, she wouldn't have had to do everything for their family on her own. Maybe then she wouldn't have gotten sick. Maybe. But he would never know, would he? He was still in contact with his kids, but that contact was restricted to occasions like birthdays, holidays, and maybe Father's Day. For the most part, he was alone except for one or two friends on the force who he talked to here and there.

There was the fishing charter idea he'd been kicking around in his head. With his pension and savings, maybe he could pull it off. Get a boat and do the damn thing. There was plenty of business on the Chesapeake during the spring, summer, and fall months. He loved to fish, and he'd always wanted a boat. Well hell, maybe he would do it. Either way, he'd cross that bridge when he got to it. And he would get to it soon enough.

CHAPTER 15

After almost another thirty minutes, Fred saw a pair of headlights edge around the corner and begin heading up the street towards where he was parked. Damn rookie. Fred was almost too angry for words. Almost. He was going to give the youngster a piece of his mind tonight, that was for damn sure.

He took one last pull from his cigarette and flicked the butt to the ground. Then he forced down the last of his cold coffee. As the car got closer, Fred pushed himself up off of the cruiser's hood and opened its passenger-side front door. He placed his black thermos inside his blue duffle and zipped the bag closed. Then he lifted the bag off of the front seat and hefted it up on his shoulder as he closed the car door behind him.

The rain had picked up and it now fell in heavy, steady drops. The pale half-moon that was sitting overhead earlier had retreated behind a patch of thick, gray cloud cover, making it even darker in the empty parking lot. The car inched forward, moving at a slow, deliberate pace towards where Fred stood.

It was bad enough that Riley was late, but now he was out here playing games? It was too late, and Fred was too tired for this shit. He might be old and washed-up, but he wasn't no damn play-toy. It was time for him and the kid to come to an understanding of how this thing worked.

He'd been too nice to the youngster. That was part of the problem right there. Constantly letting him slide and covering for him just made things worse. The boy needed to understand that he's an officer in the MPD, not some minimum wage mall security guard. This was the police force for the Nation's Capital and wasn't nobody playing games out here in these streets.

Riley didn't see this right now, but he would soon and if he wanted to survive, he had better get his shit correct. Otherwise, he wouldn't be long for this job. Maybe not this world even.

Fred didn't want to see that happen to the kid. He'd seen other youngsters with no discipline not last long on the job. They had come in with their heads not screwed on right, thinking it was all a game. Knuckleheads who were happy just to have a badge, a gun, and a license to kick some ass. The streets chewed them up and spit 'em back out. And out the door they had gone, some vertical, some horizontal, but all of them broken and ruined and then forgotten.

At last, the car crept into the parking lot. It wasn't the usual rover vehicle that the department allowed officers to use to transition between shifts. Instead, it looked to be a dark blue or black sedan, a Mercury maybe.

This was exactly the shit that Fred was talking about. The kid knew they weren't supposed to drive their POVs out here. What the hell was wrong with this idiot? Was he hardheaded or just plain dumb? And how the hell had he made it out of the academy? Did he expect Fred to drive his car back to the station, or did he think he would be able to do his shift using his POV? *No way in hell on both counts*, Fred thought to himself.

The car stopped just short of where Fred was parked, but the lights stayed on and the engine remained running. The windows were up, but Fred could hear the muffled rap music booming from the car. Exasperated, Fred threw his hands up in the air, all of his patience long gone now.

He adjusted his duffle on his shoulder and began walking towards the long sedan. The car's high beams were on, and he had to raise his hand to shield his eyes from the blinding blue-white light.

"Riley, what the hell you doing?!" Fred called out. "Come on man, stop messin' around. It's too late for this bullshit tonight. Get your ass on out here!"

Damn dumb-ass kid thought everything was a joke. Thought everything was a game. Well, Fred needed to get on home. Get a meal, a hot shower, and get his ass to bed. He may not have much of a life anymore, but it was still his life.

The car hadn't budged, and the kid hadn't shown himself. Fred imagined him sitting inside laughing his silly ass off. That's right, asshole, go ahead and laugh at the old man whose glory days are all in the rearview mirror. Soon enough you'll be like me. Best days a distant memory, and each new day dragging by without anything to look forward to anymore.

Fred reached the driver's side of the car and tried to peek into the window. The kid had illegal tint on his ride. Just another thing he'd have to talk to him about. He could make out a few lights from the dashboard and stereo, but not much else. He knocked hard on the dark window, but all he received in response was the steady pounding of the music's heavy bass.

He started to knock again but stopped himself when he realized that something wasn't right here. Instincts born from all of his years of police work kicked in and the hairs on the back of his neck stood at attention.

He remembered the kid recently talking about his beat-up Toyota Corolla and how he couldn't afford to replace it any time soon. He also remembered the kid complaining about his money troubles on a few other occasions. No way he could own this souped-up ride, right? With its nice paint, shiny rims, and sound system. No way he could afford all of that, not legally anyway. No, something wasn't jivin' here at all.

Alarms went off in Fred's head, internal warnings that told him he was in trouble. He stepped backward from the Mercury, dropped his bag, and started to reach for his service pistol. But the old patrolman was too late. He was always too late, wasn't he? Too late to make something of his career. Too late for his kids. Too late for his Meggy. Just too damn late.

Fred stumbled as his feet became tangled in the straps of his duffle bag. He felt his hands graze the butt of his pistol, but his weary, high-mileage bones were no longer up to the task. His once cat-like reflexes were now turtle-slow.

The tinted driver's side window of the sedan eased down, and Fred saw the barrel of a semi-automatic rifle emerge from the darkness. Before he could completely register what he was seeing, the semi-automatic came to life and its muzzle erupted, sending a barrage of death in his direction. He didn't see or hear the shots, but he felt the rounds tear into his body.

Pain, like red-hot metal and razor-sharp glass, ripped through Fred. He felt his back slam into the ground, felt the breath rush from his lungs, and then suddenly, just like that...he didn't feel anything anymore.

His eyes remained open and his vision started to blur, but he could still make out the moon. It had reappeared from behind the clouds accompanied by a few twinkling stars. Right then, Fred thought that this was one of the most beautiful things he'd ever seen.

Then, just as quickly as it had vanished, the pain returned with all the fury of an enemy looking for payback. Fred's chest felt caved-in, heavy like someone had placed a fifty-pound dumbbell on his solar plexus. He tasted metal as thick, sticky blood pooled in his mouth. His breath abandoned him, slipping away like a runaway lover in the night.

Fred's remaining moments of life came in a few short, ragged breaths and spasmed shudders and twitches. And then, as it was with death, there wasn't anything left. Blackness intruded from the edges of his vision and consumed him. As he lay dying, Fred had the strangest of thoughts: *What the hell happened to Riley?*

Then came the more sensible thoughts: *Meggy-baby, I've missed you so much.*

He thought about his kids and how he'd never been a good father to them. Then he thought about his many sins and secrets and how they had probably condemned him to burn in an eternal hell. How those sins and secrets outweighed any of the good he'd ever done in his life. Not that he'd done a bunch of good anyway.

I always told myself that I was a good man, but I been doin' dirt and lyin' to myself my whole damn life. I hurt so many and I've got so much blood on my hands. But now, that blood belongs to me.

Fred had always known he would have to answer for his sins, either in this life or the next. But he never thought it would come back on him like this, being shot down in the street guarding a few ramshackle buildings. Hadn't losing his family been enough?

No, he supposed, *that hadn't been nearly enough.*

There would never be enough to atone for the things he'd done. The lives he'd helped destroy. The money he'd gained through ill-gotten means. The people he'd hurt and the pain he'd caused. The sheer evil of the sins he'd committed. Little kids, for God's sake. He'd hurt children. He'd justified his actions by reasoning it had all been for his own family, but that was no excuse.

Fred was a God-fearing man, so he knew what awaited him on the other side. His death tonight was just the beginning, and he knew he deserved this and whatever followed.

As he closed his eyes for the last time, a strange calmness settled over him. His pain ceased to exist along with the rest of his world. And then, it was all black and all gone, and the man called "Slick" by his friends, family, and fellow officers was no more.

CHAPTER 16

He is wrath...

And so, it begins. His endgame is underway, and everything is playing out just as he's planned it. After all the years spent in shadows, forced to endure an agonizing waiting game, he is ready to exact his revenge. He's spent so much time watching and planning, going over the details again and again while waiting for the perfect opportunity to reveal itself.

He's planned for every eventuality, every inevitability, and possibility. His moment is now and he's going to seize it by the throat with both hands. Then he'll refuse to let go until he chokes the life from it. He'll set things right without anything or anyone getting in his way. He's waited too long for this to go any other way.

He will end those responsible for destroying his life... at any cost. He isn't a monster like the men he's hunting. He isn't anything like them, and he proved that last night when he showed mercy to the young police officer.

The old man's relief had been late and that had helped set the stage for last night's events. After taking the younger cop by surprise, he spared the man's life and left him unconscious in his vehicle. He probably awoke to a bad headache and a bruised ego, but he'd live to see another day.

The same couldn't be said for the old man. Fred Mooney had represented evil beyond words. He did the world a service last night by ridding it of that evil.

He saw the shock and fear register in Mooney's eyes as he pulled the trigger and sent the old man to hell. And with that shock and fear, there was also a look that said the old man knew that his past sins had finally caught up to him.

There's no mistaking the look of reckoning in someone's eyes as they recall their life during the last moments of their existence. That look on the old man's face made all the time he'd invested well worth it.

For years, he kept a close watch over his victim. He bird-dogged him from a distance, breaking down his habits, his predictabilities. He studied

Mooney's professional and personal lives. He knew about the death of Mooney's wife. And as far as he was concerned, that was just a small portion of the price Mooney needed to pay.

He took a man's life last night, there was no denying that. But he wasn't the one who light this fire. That happened years ago on a cold, tragic evening when two little boys were just trying to make it home from school. Instead, they became the victims of monsters. Now, he will be the one to make sure this fire stays lit and burns bright until there is nothing left but ashes.

He isn't claiming innocence in this; he won't dare do that. But his targets committed unspeakable atrocities long before he began gunning down policemen. He's seen some of those atrocities with his own eyes. His innocence, along with his dreams, was stolen away from him all those many years ago. No one is innocent in this game of death, not him and especially not the men he is hunting.

Officer Mooney won't be the last life he extinguishes. No way. With each name he crosses off his list, he gets closer to the retribution he's waited almost a lifetime to obtain. He will hunt down each of his targets, and he'll make them pay for what they did to him, to his family, and other innocents like him. The other men on his list don't know it yet, but just like Mooney, they'll find out soon enough that he's booked a reservation in hell with each of their names on it.

CHAPTER 17

Detective Darius Cole wanted to smash his phone. He knew that the smarter, less expensive option would be to simply turn it off. But right now, he wanted to place the Samsung on his desk and use his fist to hammer it into small pieces.

That was the kind of mood arguing with a crazy person put you in. And Sienna was definitely crazy, and she definitely loved to argue. The damn girl even loved to argue via text message. He'd found that out early on in their...what was this thing they were doing with each other? Hell, could he even call it a relationship? He didn't think so. He didn't know what to call it, but this wasn't a relationship.

He'd known Sienna less than three months. They hung out on occasion and had even hooked up a handful of times. Good times, he had to admit, but not like dates or anything close to that. What they shared was more like a late night "show me yours and I'll show you mine and let's make each other feel good" type of deal. And that right there was the source of their dysfunction.

They obviously saw this situation as two completely different things. Sienna wanted to transform their situation into something it clearly wasn't and, in his eyes, never would be. When he met Sienna, they agreed to have a little bit of fun. They both claimed that they weren't looking for anything serious. No commitment, no stress. All fun and all good.

Now, Sienna wanted to change the rules of their game and had been pressing him to commit to a monogamous relationship. She wanted him to meet her five-year-old daughter and go to cookouts with her family, but he wasn't having any of that action.

He'd calmly explained his feelings to Sienna and even reminded her of their original conversation and understanding. Like a fool, he'd hoped this would help Sienna see reason and they could continue their "friendship" without any more drama. Instead, the conversation had the opposite effect and had pissed Sienna off.

But, instead of saying the hell with him and moving on, Sienna had dug her heels in further and continued to press him about their situation. She alternated between wanting to spend the night with him and accusing him of using her for sex. Today's argument had been more of the same, Sienna pressuring him to give her something he didn't have to offer.

Sienna was beautiful and the sex was damn good, better than good, but she was also clearly out of her mind. He knew he should cut her off completely. In fact, he'd tried to do just that a couple of months ago, and that attempt had failed miserably. The damn girl was like an incurable disease or something. She wouldn't go away, despite him telling her they didn't want the same thing. She just kept coming back stronger.

Like all of their other "discussions," the one today had been an exercise in futility. Her latest text message had read: *"F U Darius!"* This type of communication was typical of Sienna whenever she lost her temper. He was used to her talking to him this way by now, but it still set him off. He didn't understand why Sienna didn't just walk away. Hell, he didn't understand why *he* didn't just walk away.

So, Sienna kept hanging around and he kept letting her. They would argue, she would cry and tell him to leave her alone and have a "blessed life", which actually meant "go straight to hell!" And he would do just that, refusing to call or text her. Then she would reappear, they would do their normal "midnight make-up" thing, and then the cycle would start all over again. *What kind of stupid, silly shit was that?*

His phone vibrated again and he reached for it, but he was interrupted by someone yelling his name from the other side of the squad room. That someone was his lieutenant. He glanced at the digital clock on his phone. It read 9:30 a.m. He'd been at work for almost two hours and hadn't done a damn thing but wage another text message war with a woman he was sleeping with on just a semi-regular basis.

"Cole!" the LT's voice boomed again. "My office! Let's go! Get in here! *Now!*"

Cole pushed his seat away from his desk. He grabbed his blazer off the back of the chair and his cell phone off his desk and started towards the LT's office. He knew what was coming. He'd spent the last twelve months as a homicide detective, and he'd done this walk enough to know what was up. In a city like D.C., there was always a high priority case. And too often that case was a homicide.

First thing this morning, he'd heard about the patrolman who'd been gunned down late last night. Of course, he'd heard about it; everyone had. The entire precinct was buzzing, but Cole had been consumed with his own problems.

This was the second cop shooting in the last two months. Brothers in blue who'd lost their lives in the line of duty. He hadn't worked with the old guy, but he'd heard the guys around the precinct talking about how close he'd been to retirement.

Public sentiment across the country had turned against law enforcement in a major way. Not that it had ever been favorable, but it was as bad now as ever. The word "police" was a four-letter word in the eyes of many citizens who felt that law enforcement often abused its power and exceeded its legal mandate.

People were tired of hearing about young black men being gunned down at the hands of policemen who seemed to operate above the law without consequence. No one cared anymore if the kills were righteous or not. Even worse, there were people out there looking for payback, and they were willing to commit murder themselves to get it.

There had been the Dallas shooter not too long ago who'd gunned down five officers and wounded nine others. Incidents like these were starting to occur with an increased frequency all over the country. Now, two cops had been murdered here in the Nation's Capital. The mayor, the chief of police, and the media were demanding answers, but so far, the MPD was coming up empty.

Cole stopped about halfway across the squad room, turned around and walked back to his desk. He picked up the large paper cup filled with the herbal tea and honey mix he'd been nursing for the last hour. He took a sip. Lukewarm. Good enough. No need in going into a possible ass-chewing without his cup of morning tea.

"We have a cop-killer on our hands, Detective," the LT announced as Cole entered his office. "Maybe a serial cop-killer at that. Two of our boys have been hit now."

No shit, Sherlock, Cole thought to himself.

Chief of Detectives Lieutenant Ramon Hernandez III was a walking, talking cliché if Cole had ever seen one. The short, pudgy man was straight out of a bad action-comedy cop movie. Everything from his surly personality, thinning hair, and potbelly to his sweat-stained faded white shirt and, of course, the cigar he was always chewing on.

"Yes sir," Cole replied as he took a seat in the burgundy cracked leather chair positioned in front of the LT's cluttered desk. "He hit one of us last night. Read about it this morning."

"Damn right he did," Hernandez said as he rolled the edges of his thick mustache between his left forefinger and thumb. "And this time he hit one from our precinct. Patrolman Fred Mooney. Old-timer. Been with the force since forever. Damn good man. You know him?"

"No sir, never had the pleasure." That was mostly true. He hadn't worked with Mooney and had never even spoken to him, but he was familiar with the patrolman and those like him.

In his heyday, Mooney had been part of the old-guard; hard-nosed cops who believed the rules didn't apply to them and routinely operated outside of the lines of the law. They believed in the "shoot first and ask questions later" mantra. Cole despised that generation of police and everything it stood for. Mooney and those like him were responsible for the stereotype that today's policemen had to endure.

Part of the reason Cole had joined the force was to help change how things were done and how the public viewed the MPD. He'd been naive in that thought. He knew now that it would take more than just one man to institute the kind of change needed around here. It also didn't help that many of today's officers chose to keep those stereotypes alive and well by doing their best to live up to them.

"Well, he was one of ours," the LT continued. "A patrolman pulling mid-shifts and keeping watch on an abandoned industrial park. Just riding out the rest of his time until retirement, and some sonofabitch ambushed him."

"How did it happen, sir?" Cole asked. "What do we know so far?"

"His relief was late," Hernandez replied as he shook his head. "Some shit-for-brains rookie named Riley. Turns out the shooter surprised Riley and put him out of commission. Left him unconscious and tied-up in his vehicle before he took Mooney out. When Riley came to, he got loose and went to his post. That's where he found Mooney's body. IA's already involved, checking out Riley's story now. This happened right in our backyard. So, you know what that means right, Cole?"

Cole paused before answering, not because he was thinking about his answer, but because he figured this was part of the script.

"Yes sir," he said. "Means it's our turn now."

"Damn right, Cole," the LT said as he leaned forward and placed both of his hands flat on his desk. "Up until now, we've been lending support to the other precincts working this case. But, with this latest hit being in our district, we're running point now. The order came down from on high first thing this morning. And...I want you on this one."

"Me, sir?" Cole asked with genuine surprise and pointed at his own chest. "You want *me* working *this* case?"

"Hell, not as the lead," the LT laughed and tapped the ashes from his cigar into a nearby ashtray. "Don't go gettin' your nuts all swollen, son. Landry and Jacobs are running point. You'll be their support. They're the senior detectives in homicide, and you know they close the shit out of cases. So, it's their show. But I want you running backup for them."

Cole understood now. He was going to be their errand boy. He would do the grunt work. He would eat the leftover scraps while they got to feed on the meat of the case. Here he was thinking that his time had come to get off the bench and get in the game. But he knew this was just fool's gold.

He also knew Tony "Big T" Landry and Mark "Mayday" Jacobs, and he didn't like them at all. The two senior detectives were just that, a couple of senior dicks. They were part of the same old guard as Fred Mooney. The pair had high case closure rates, and they knew they were among the best on the entire force. They peacocked around the station like they owned the place.

Cole figured they pretty much did own the place with all the favor they had earned with the senior brass. They drove the best vehicles, did the most press, and worked the most glamorous cases. Cole was sure that the LT figured he was doing him a favor by allowing him to be Landry's and Jacobs' errand runner. And he was right.

Cole had been a mediocre cop at best during his few years on the force. Sure, he'd made detective and closed a few cases here and there, but it had all been basic cop work and he hadn't invested much effort into it at all. So, Hernandez had yet to trust him with anything big. He was still fairly green for a detective and hadn't been in Homicide long enough for anyone to give a shit about him or his career.

"Look, Cole," the LT said like he was able to read his mind, "I'm doing you a favor here. This is some good shit that I'm handing you, ok? You get to get your dick wet with our A-Team, play with the varsity squad. You can learn how to some actual cop work; and who knows, if you help them solve this case, this could be a big break for you. Like I said, I'm gifting you an opportunity that you didn't earn. So, don't shit in my hand, rookie. You got me?"

Cole had to admit that the pudgy bastard made a good point. He hadn't done much in the way of good cop work recently. When he'd joined the force, he'd had his own reasons for wanting to be a cop; but lately, he couldn't help but wonder about the point of it all. Maybe this was the opportunity he'd been waiting on.

"Yes sir," Cole said straightening his back and sitting up in the chair. "I'm on it. Thank you for your confidence. When do I start?"

"Good man," Hernandez said and stabbed out the last of his cigar. "Jacobs and Landry are already out working the scene. I wanted to speak with you first, but you can go catch up to them now. I'll text you the address." The LT picked up his cell phone and began typing.

A few moments later Cole felt his cell vibrate. He rose and moved towards the office door.

"Oh, and Detective," Hernandez called behind him. He turned and saw that the man had already grabbed another cigar from his desk and was using his cigar cutter to prep it for smoking.

"Sir?"

"Just follow Landry and Jacobs, alright? Do what they say, and everything will be fine."

"Yes sir," he replied and nodded at the Lieutenant before he exited the office.

Just go get the coffee, donuts, and sandwiches and stay your silly ass out of the way, Cole. That was what the LT had really just told him, but Cole had other plans.

CHAPTER 18

Cole pulled out of the station and steered his unmarked cruiser through the last of rush hour traffic on Bladensburg Road. He missed almost every green light along his route. At each stop he watched the civilians going about their day-to-day business without a care in the world. Cole envied these people.

The air had a cold snap to it this morning, and the sky rolled over on itself in a cloudy gray for as far as Cole could see. The sun had taken a sick day, and its absence served as a reminder of how rapidly winter was approaching.

The weather also made him think of Christmas. It was less than a week away and he hadn't even noticed. Not that he would. He'd stopped celebrating that holiday and any other holiday a long time ago. He maintained a solitary existence and he liked it that way. So, in spite of Sienna's insistence that they should be celebrating Christmas together, Cole didn't have plans to do any Christmas shopping. His Christmas would consist of a quiet night at home with dinner for one. And that was a good thing given the current shape of his bank and credit card accounts.

Almost twenty minutes after he left the Fifth District Station, Cole pulled his department-issued vehicle into a run-down industrial park on Adams Place. Dingy red brick buildings filled the cramped area. Their brown and gray garage doors were dented and showed signs of heavy rust and disrepair. The glass storefronts and windows of some of the buildings were either cracked or broken out altogether.

Cole wondered why the city would waste the time, money, and manpower trying to save this eyesore. But since the city's officials had chosen to spare the industrial park from complete demolition, they were forced to keep a police presence nearby to deter the drug trafficking, prostitution, and squatting that usually gravitated to this type of area.

The crime scene was in the center of the industrial park near a gravel-covered parking lot. The area had been taped off with the standard yellow crime scene tape. Most of the regular crime scene participants had cleared out by now and just a few techs, policemen, and members of the media continued to linger around the perimeter.

Jacobs and Landry stood next to each other on the outside of the taped barrier. Both men were heavyset with broad shoulders and equally broad waistlines. Each stood an inch or two taller than Cole at around six foot or so, with Landry being the slightly taller of the pair.

Both men looked to be in their mid-fifties, but Cole knew that Landry was in his late thirties. Cole wondered what kind of hard and fast living the younger man had done to age that rapidly.

Jacobs' blonde hair had gone mostly gray, and he kept it in a tightly buzzed crew cut around his red, line-creased face. Landry wore his dark brown hair a little longer than his partner, but not by much. The hair around his temples was gray, and his skin sported the same weathered and sun-reddened hue as Jacobs.

The pair also looked like they shopped at the same low budget clothing store. Jacobs' suit was the color of a brown food stain and fit him like...well it didn't fit him at all. It just hung baggy in some places and bunched up and stretched out in others. Landry wasn't in any better shape with his own wrinkled charcoal suit. Both men sported white shirts that hadn't seen bleach or an iron lately. Their ties sported ugly patterns and had been knotted haphazardly.

"Well, well, well, look who it is," Landry said when he saw Cole approaching. "Hey Jake, man, look who it is: our man Mr. Green himself. What's up, rookie?"

Jacobs looked at Cole with disgust and said, "Hell you doing here? You lost, Cole? Or you come to see how the big boys earn their pay? Oh wait, maybe he brought us some coffee and donuts, Land. That it, Cole? You on a coffee run?" The two men laughed and high-fived.

"What's up, Detective?" Cole responded, not flinching at their insults.

He pretended to be numb to how the other detectives in the squad treated him, knowing that if he reacted or tried to discourage it, things would get worse. It had been this way since he became a detective and had been assigned to the homicide unit. In their eyes, he was an outsider, a rookie who had been gifted a promotion he hadn't earned. They didn't want or need him on their team. Cole figured that one day he would earn the respect of his fellow officers, but if that day never came, then he would be fine with that, too.

Jacobs, still laughing at his joke, said, "Oh come on Cole, don't be that way. We're just fuckin' with you, son. How about we start over?"

He held up his meaty right hand to offer Cole a high five, "What up, yo, gimme some!"

Cole wanted to punch the bigger man square in his fat face. Instead, he ignored the detective and his attempt at comedy and moved past him to get a closer look at the crime scene.

"Come on, don't leave me hangin', bro," Jacobs called from behind him. "What? No high five? What up with that, homeslice?"

Landry, standing a few feet away, continued to laugh. Cole stepped past him as well and ducked under the yellow crime scene tape. The body had already been moved to the coroner's office, but the white chalk outline of the victim remained. Pools of dried blood stained several spots in and around the outline. Cole could clearly see how the patrolman's body had been found. Lying on his back, his arms and legs askew.

Cole turned and looked at Jacobs and Landry who had both remained outside of the yellow-taped border.

"I heard Mooney was almost a forty-year vet on the verge of retirement." Cole asked, "Either of you know him?"

"Yeah, I knew him. What's it to you?" Jacobs said, the playfulness gone from his voice now. "He was one of my first partners back when I was a narc. Damn good man, damn good cop. We did jump-out together. One of the best cops I ever worked with. Didn't deserve this shit here."

"Well," Cole said and looked Jacobs square in the eye as the corner of his mouth turned upwards into a small smile, "I guess at least one person thought he deserved it."

"What you say, rookie?" Jacobs said and started walking towards him, but Landry caught the big man and held him back. They weren't laughing now, were they?

Cole didn't budge. He welcomed the scrap, even though he knew it could lead to a suspension, or worse, for him.

"What? No jokes for me now, *yo*?" Cole said as he turned and walked away from the two older cops. "I'll start the canvass. Check and see if anyone saw anything."

"Hey, to hell with you, Cole! You keep walking! That's right, get your ass outta here. Slick Mooney was more of a cop than you'll ever be," Jacobs called behind him as he strained against Landry's hold. "So, you can go fuck yourself, you prick!"

CHAPTER 19

Washington, D.C.—circa the early 2010s...

Today should've been a great day for Scoop. One of the best of his young life, in fact. But it wasn't. Here he was graduating from college near the top of his class, but all he could think about were the missing pieces of his life. Throughout the Howard University auditorium moms, dads, and other family members clapped, hollered, and shed tears of joy as they watched their family members receive their respective degrees. It was almost a perfect scene and a perfect day. Almost. But there was just one problem. The seats reserved for Scoop's family were empty.

There was no one there to clap and call Scoop's name as he walked across the stage to receive his bachelor's degree in criminal justice. His older brother was all the family he had left, and he'd been nowhere to be found for the last couple of weeks. As was his routine, he'd disappeared and hadn't called or answered his cell phone. Scoop didn't know if his brother even had a cell phone anymore. And although Scoop had known his brother wouldn't show today, he'd held out hope until the last possible second.

Their parents had been gone for a number of years now. Beanie's issues had taken a toll on their marriage. They had tried to make it work but when it had become clear that there was no hope for Beanie, their mother had left all of them for a new life and she hadn't looked back. Scoop had never tried to contact or locate her; and to this day, he didn't know where she was or if she was even alive. He didn't hate her, but he didn't feel the need to have her in his life anymore. If she didn't care, then why should he?

And their dad, well he'd tried to cope, hadn't he? But his coping mechanism had ended up being the bottle, and cirrhosis and a heart attack had taken his life just a few years later. He'd died a miserable death, the alcohol and heartbreak each taking their own heavy toll.

After the ceremony concluded, Scoop treated himself to a celebratory dinner from a local

Chinese carryout. Then he'd headed back to his small off-campus apartment to eat and change out of his cap, gown, and suit. Instead of hooking up with some of his classmates to continue the celebration, Scoop made other plans for his evening.

He changed into a black sweat suit, grabbed the small Smith and Wesson .380 he kept hidden in his room and went back out to look for his older brother. His company that night would be the compact pistol concealed in the deep pockets of his sweatpants. This was a sad, but all too familiar routine that Scoop had performed too many times to count.

He began his search for Beanie by visiting the street corners and other drug hot spots that his brother frequented. He knew almost all the dealers, and they usually let him pass through without any problems. Some even told him when they had last seen Beanie.

A few hours passed and after tracking down a few of his brother's fellow addicts, Scoop found himself in an abandoned section of a run-down housing project not far from the Minnesota Avenue metro station on the Northeast side of the city. He'd checked with almost everyone he knew that might know of his brother's whereabouts and had been pointed to this location.

Night had fallen, but the sun had left behind a thick, suffocating blanket of humidity. Pungent, stomach-churning smells assaulted Scoop's nose as soon as he exited his tan Ford Taurus and began climbing the stairs to the first tenement. The funk of body odor, urine, feces...and death...was so strong that Scoop almost turned around and abandoned his search. Instead, he pressed on, trying his best to breathe through his mouth as he made his way past the front entrance of the first building. He moved deeper into the darkness, using a small pocket flashlight to guide his steps.

The first two buildings had been empty and, again, he'd been about to give up his search. But, as Scoop entered the third and last building in the section, he found that it was a nesting-ground for dope fiends. He stepped over and around addict after addict and checked each floor and room, working his way towards the top floor of the four-story dump.

There had been no sign of his older brother among the numerous drugged-out zombies. He'd tried to think of that as a good thing. The "no news is good news logic." But, on the third floor of the abandoned building, Scoop's good news theory vanished.

He stepped into a pitch-black room, and at first, he thought the room was empty like some of the others. Relief flowed over him. He was about to leave the room when his light passed over something, rather, over someone. And that's when he saw him. He saw his brother.

There was Beanie, slumped in a far corner of the room, all alone. Scoop could see the effect the drugs had taken on his brother's malnourished frame. He lay there, unmoving, wearing nothing but his pants. His shirt, shoes, and socks were gone. The momentary relief Scoop had felt just minutes earlier was now replaced by a deep and resigned sadness. He was face-to-face with his biggest fear.

The dirty ripped blue jeans Beanie wore had fallen well below his waist exposing protruding hip bones and his other private parts. Scoop observed the track marks running up and down his brother's arms and in-between the toes on his bare feet. A painful hollowness expanded deep in the pit of Scoop's stomach, and long overdue tears made their way to the surface.

Hot tears stung Scoop's eyes and blurred his vision. His heart hurt deep in his chest. He wanted to scream, he wanted to howl, and he wanted to turn and run away from this horrible nightmare. Instead, he kneeled and placed his fingers on Beanie's carotid artery. As expected, Scoop didn't find a pulse. Any fool could see that his brother had been dead for some time now.

The stench of Beanie's voided bowels filled the room and answered the question as to why the thieves hadn't bothered to take his jeans. His cloudy, dead eyes and the needle stuck in the crook of his left arm told the tragic narrative of Beanie's demise.

Scoop's older brother and childhood idol had overdosed and killed himself in that filthy dope house. But the truth of it all was that he'd died many years ago on the day those cops snatched him off that street corner. That day had truly been the last day of Beanie's short life; everything after that had just served to delay the inevitable. Scoop hadn't comprehended any of this until right now as he stood over his brother's drug-abused corpse.

CHAPTER 20

Present Day…

Cole canvassed the area for a grand total of one whole hour, which had yielded zero leads and had been a complete waste of time. He'd spoken to a few people who lived a few blocks from the crime scene. As he'd expected, no one saw anything.

In fact, of the twenty or so doors he knocked on, just a handful of the residents even bothered to answer and speak with him. Before he began the canvass, he'd been sure that no one had seen anything related to the shooting. Even if someone had seen something, they wouldn't be willing to talk to the police. But that wasn't anything new, was it? No one ever wanted to talk to police.

From an investigator's perspective, there were obvious fundamental flaws in trying to obtain information on this crime by canvassing the locals.

For one, this crime was committed in the late-night hours in a very secluded and empty industrial area. And two, policemen were seen by many as the enemy. And three, for all Cole knew the people in this area viewed this cop-killer as some sort of Robin Hood, standing up for the common man and all that good stuff.

Some of these people were more likely to help hide the shooter's identity instead of helping the police catch him. Fight the power and stand up to the man. Cole could hear Public Enemy's socially-conscious classic, "Fight the Power," bumping in his head. He could also hear NWA's incendiary hit, "Fuck tha Police," bumping around in there, too.

Cole decided he'd wasted enough time and was returning to his car when a loud noise coming from behind him caught his attention. The noise sounded like someone tapping on a window and was coming from one of the apartment buildings he'd just exited.

He turned, looked up, and saw a teenage girl standing in the second-floor window of one of the homes he'd already visited. She had a panicked look on her face and was waving to get his attention. When she saw Cole looking up at her, she pointed to the alley adjacent to her building and then she vanished from the window.

The alleyway the teenager had pointed him towards was narrow and dark, but it had an opening on both ends. As Cole approached the alley, he wondered if this was a setup and if he was about to become a victim himself. Maybe the girl was working with the shooter and meant to lure Cole into the alley for an ambush. He moved his right hand to his hip and unsnapped his holster's retention strap.

The girl from the window appeared in the alley, emerging from what Cole assumed was her building's rear entrance. She had a worried expression on her face as she nervously waved for him to come towards her. Cole checked his surroundings to see if he was being watched or if any new vehicles or people had shown up to the scene. Then, slowly, he entered the alley.

The teenager, who couldn't be more than fifteen, was a jitterbug. She was tall for her age and skinny, with coffee brown skin about the same shade as Cole's and two long braids that hung down behind her shoulders. Cole could see that normally she was a nice-looking kid, but right now her face was twisted into a hard frown. Her eyes were wide, and they darted back and forth, and every few seconds, she looked over her shoulder. Cole couldn't help but wonder if she was high on something or just scared...like him. His hand gravitated towards his pistol again, but he caught himself. He didn't want to scare her off without seeing exactly what she wanted.

She must have noticed his hand because her eyes grew even bigger and she took a step back.

"Whoa," he said, holding up his hands, palms out. "Sorry about that. Dark alley and all, ya know? But it's cool. It's all good. We're good, right?"

The girl didn't speak, but she nodded and remained in place. She was wringing her hands and shifting her weight from one foot to the other.

"So, what's going on?" Cole asked, looking around to make sure they were still alone. "Everything ok? You seemed pretty excited at the window up there."

"I n-needed to t-talk to you and I didn't w-want you to drive away," the girl said, her words leaving her voice box in a chopped-up stutter. "S-sorry if I scared you. Y-you looking for whoever killed that cop, right?"

"Yeah, I am. That's exactly what I'm doing," Cole said taking a small step forward, definitely interested now. "Someone murdered that policeman last night. In fact, two policemen have been killed recently, and we think they may have been related. You know anything about these crimes? You see something?"

"I-I might," she said. "Well, I'm not sure 'cause I didn't see anything, but...but, I think I might know something."

"Ok, listen. I want you to take a breath and try to calm down, alright? You're ok here with me. What's your name?" Cole asked.

She did as she was told and took in a long deep breath and blew it out slowly. She seemed to calm some, but she hesitated a moment longer as if she wasn't sure about giving Cole her name. Then she said, "Jessie, my name is Jessie."

"Hi Jessie, my name is Detective Cole. Do you live here?"

"Yeah. Me and my family stay up there in apartment 201. Me, my momma, my dad, and my two brothers."

"Ok. So that was your mom I spoke to earlier when I knocked on your door?"

"Yeah, that was her, but she don't know nothin'. So, what she told you was true."

"Ok, I feel that. So, what is it that you know, Jessie?"

"Well," she said, hesitating again as if just speaking the words might end her life right then and there, "I think I might know who shot that cop last night."

CHAPTER 21

Jessie's words were a game changer and immediately turned a waste of a day into possibly a huge break for Cole. He tried to contain his excitement, but his heart was thudding hard against the inside of his chest.

"Ok, how do you know that?" he asked, careful not to sound too anxious. "Did you see something?"

"Nah, I already told you I didn't see nothin', but I may have heard somethin'."

"Heard what?" he asked, suspicious now. His excitement started to wane just a bit.

"Look, I didn't hear the shootin' or anything like that. I just may have heard something about it, ok?"

Cole wanted to tell the girl to cut the crap and spit it out already, but he knew how this had to go.

Slow and easy, at the witness' pace and comfort level.

"Ok, Jessie, so what did you hear?"

"I heard this boy that lives in my building talking some trash about it to his homeboys. The walls in this building are thin and sometimes I like to keep my window open 'cause the radiator makes my room too hot."

"I hear ya," Cole said, understanding exactly what that was like. "Go on."

"So, yeah, I heard him braggin' about how he shot somebody last night. They were right out there talking in fact," she said and pointed to the rear of the alley.

"My room is just up there above it so I can hear most of what people say down there. They always hangin' out back there drinkin' and smokin' and being all loud. Sometimes, my momma calls the police when they get too out-of-hand."

Cole looked in the direction she was pointing. The spot was secluded from the main street and made for a decent hangout spot if the weather was good.

He turned his attention back to Jessie and she continued with her story. "He said he smoked some old dude who looked like police. Said he was high, and he just walked up to the old dude and put a bullet in him just for the fun of it. I heard him talkin' about it this morning when I was gettin' dressed to walk my youngest brother to summer camp."

"About what time was this?"

"About eight-thirty, I suppose. Close to it. Supposed to have my brother to camp by nine."

"Kind of early for the knuckleheads to be up, ain't it?"

"Not when there's trouble to get into. They always braggin' about how they gotta 'rise and grind' to get that money."

"Rise and grind, huh? Ok. What's his name? The dude you heard bragging about the shooting?"

"His name is Rome. Well, Jerome. But everyone calls him Rome. And he's no good."

"Have you seen Rome since this morning, Jessie?" Cole asked looking up at the building.

"I think he's home. I heard him tell his boys that he was going to lie low today and wait and see what the news said about last night."

Cole looked at the girl, searching her eyes for any sign that she wasn't being straight up with him. He found none.

"Jessie, why are you helping me? Most people around here don't talk to the cops."

"I don't talk to cops. Can't trust y'all. Plus, you can get yourself killed that way. But I'm doing it this time because of my little brothers. Rome is dangerous and just all around bad. Always has been since we were little. He's always getting into shit. I don't want him around my little brothers. He been trying to get my middle brother, Troy, to work for him. I figure me telling you will help with that problem. But you can't tell nobody I told you. You can't. People find out and I'm good as dead. Hear me? Dead."

Cole understood exactly what she meant and he said, "I hear you, Jessie. What you're doing is very brave. But if I use this information to arrest Rome, I can't promise that I'll be able to keep your name out of it. You're a key witness and you could be called to testify in court about what you heard this morning."

He honestly didn't know how admissible her witness account would be in court with her being a minor and her parents not being present, but he wanted to be straight with her before acting on what she'd told him.

Jessie seemed to consider what he told her, and he could see the fear growing in her eyes as she ran through the possibilities in her mind. He thought she might back out and refuse to help him any further. But then she surprised him. Her eyes gained a look of defiance, and she pushed her shoulders back and puffed out her chest a little.

"Ok, I'll do it," she said. "For my brothers. I'll do it, but you have to promise to look out for me, ok? You have to promise."

"I got you, Jessie," he told her. "I promise we'll protect you. And thank you, Jessie. Thank you for being so brave. Now, I need to know where Rome lives and what he looks like, ok?"

Jessie told him which apartment Rome lived in on the fourth floor, and she gave him a pretty detailed physical description of the suspect.

"That's great, Jessie. You've been a big help. I may need to talk to you some more about what you heard, but we'll worry about that later, ok? For now, why don't you go on home and let me handle it from here?"

Jessie nodded and headed back towards her building while he returned to his vehicle and called in the lead. He didn't want to wait for backup. This was his opportunity and he didn't want to miss it. But he knew backup would be here soon enough, and he needed to do this by the book.

Rome could be in the wind at any time, and Cole didn't want to let that happen. But instead of doing something foolish, he went back into the alley and did his best to keep an eye on both entrances while he waited. If Rome tried to leave before then, he would grab him and hold him until backup arrived.

Jacobs and Landry arrived on the scene a few minutes later along with backup, which included members of the precinct's tactical team. Jacobs assumed command of the scene and insisted that he and Landry lead the raid. It was obvious Jacobs was trying to put Cole in his place, but none of that "no guts, no glory" crap mattered to him. He'd been the one to find the witness, locate the suspect, and call it all in. He would make sure it went in the report that way.

Jerome Watkins, better known as Rome, had indeed been home. But, when the takedown team forced their way through his front door, he wasn't inside. Someone must have tipped Rome off to the police gathering outside of his building because he'd tried to make a getaway using his building's rear laundry room exit. The same exit Jessie had used to meet Cole in the alley. However, instead of finding a clear path to freedom, Rome found Cole and several patrolmen waiting on him.

Seeing no way out and not wanting to commit suicide by cop, Rome surrendered and allowed himself to be taken into custody without issue. A search of Rome's person and his apartment yielded plenty of evidence in the form of drugs and a couple of handguns to warrant his arrest.

After the chaos and excitement of the arrest and after Cole filled a less-than-enthused Jacobs and Landry in on the details, he left the scene and headed back to the precinct. As he steered his car away from the scene, he thought about the ease with which this case had broken open for him. He knew police work wasn't always this easy, but this was more than that. The way this case had fallen into his lap and the way it had all played out. Well, to Cole it seemed more like divine intervention, though he'd never believed in that sort of thing.

PART FIVE

"YOUR LIFE IS CALLING"

CHAPTER 22

Seagulls circled outside; boisterous, fidgety, and agitated. Their loud, early morning chorus penetrated the walls of the small bedroom and dragged Judith Landry from her sleep, mercifully ending a fitful few hours of rest. Pain greeted Jude as soon as she opened her eyes. Last night had been bad. But that wasn't anything new. Almost every night was bad.

A wave of relief washed over her when she rolled over and saw the empty space next to her. The clock on her cell phone read 7:05 a.m. and Jude guessed that he'd already left for work.

Thank God, she thought. *Thank God.*

She wanted to pull the covers back over her head and try to sleep away this nightmare, but she knew she couldn't do that. Not today. Not ever, in fact.

She had responsibilities. The house needed cleaning. Groceries needed buying. Dinner needed cooking. Or else there would be consequences.

After forcing herself out of bed and showering, Jude stood in front of the bathroom mirror and took an accounting of the latest round of damage. Angry-looking, dark purple welts puckered along her arms and sides. At the sight of her black eye, swollen cheek and split bottom lip, hot tears fell from Jude's eyes.

How could this be happening to her? Even worse, how could she be allowing this to happen? She wasn't one of "those women," was she? But the bruises and scars, both old and new, internal and external, said otherwise and forced a completely different truth on her.

Ten years ago, Tony Landry came in Jude's life and stole her heart. Tall, lean, and movie-star handsome, the former college quarterback swooped in and swept Judith off of her feet. They were married after six months of dating, and Jude happily gave up her budding finance career in Corporate America to support his dream of playing professional football.

She'd been so young when they first met, barely out of college and just beginning her first job. Her family and friends warned her not to give up her own dreams, but it all seemed so right at the time. Tony promised her the world and he delivered on his promises...at least in the beginning.

Now, their dream marriage was her own personal nightmare. Tony's intensity and dark side that had once thrilled and excited Jude, now horrified and tormented her. He continued to blame her for his failed pro career. A career that hadn't amounted to anything more than him being a late-round draft pick and then bouncing around the league for a few years before it was all over. He'd never managed to stick on any team's roster for more than one season and never played in a meaningful game.

Jude had been willing to take the ride with Tony for as long as it lasted, but before they knew it his pro career had ceased to exist, and his dream of stardom and wealth was dead and gone. Word had spread through the league about his poor work ethic, bad attitude, and overall lack of talent. His opportunities dried up like a raisin in the sun, and just like that, the league was done with him. He'd hoped to get into coaching or broadcasting after his playing days were over, but the teams and the sports news outlets wanted nothing more to do with him.

He hadn't met Jude until he was near the end of his pro football flame-out, but still, he blamed her. He called her a burden and an unwanted distraction and said that if he'd spent less time focusing on her, he would've been a star in the league. He blamed her for the job he'd been forced to work after he finally gave up on football and the money ran out. He blamed her for their financial issues, although she'd tried to curb his expensive gambling and drinking habits. And even with the money gone, he wouldn't allow her to work. Worst of all, he blamed her for their inability to conceive children. Feeling boxed-in and hopeless, Tony became a miserable, destructive person who took his frustration out on Jude in the worst possible ways. And then, as if the verbal abuse hadn't been enough, Tony began physically hurting her.

CHAPTER 23

The first time Tony hit Jude, he apologized for days, begging her not to leave him. He blamed his behavior on the drinking, the stress and the money problems. He promised her over and over that it would never happen again, that he'd be the man she'd fallen in love with in the beginning.

And Jude believed him. She'd wanted to believe him and believe *in* him. She'd *needed* to believe him and believe that he could be the man of her dreams. After all, he was all she had now. She'd grown distant from her family and friends after all of the moving around before settling in the D.C. area thousands of miles from everyone and everything she knew back in Seattle.

It wasn't long before he hurt Jude again. He hit her again, and he apologized again, and Jude stayed. Again, and again. And that became their life. He'd hurt her and then he'd apologize, and she took it every time. Eventually, he stopped apologizing, but he kept on slapping, punching, and kicking her. All the while she took it and tried to ignore the pain and mounting sense of hopelessness overtaking her.

When Tony joined the police force, Jude hoped that he'd found his calling. And, at first, it appeared this was true. Tony seemed to get himself together. He stopped drinking, gambling, and even the physical and verbal abuse. He made it through the academy and graduated without issue. So what if he'd been near the bottom of his class. That didn't matter. He'd made it through. He was an officer in the Metropolitan Police Department. Jude had been so proud of him, and Tony seemed happy and content. She even allowed herself to hope that everything would be all right with them.

Tony's happiness and Jude's hopefulness had been short-lived. Long hours, low pay, and overdue bills brought reality crashing back into their lives and brought Tony's fist crashing back into Jude's body. The gambling, drinking, and abuse all returned in full force, but still, Jude stayed. What else could she do? She couldn't leave. Where would she have gone? So, she stayed.

She even stayed when she caught Tony cheating. And after a while, he no longer bothered to hide his infidelity from her. Yet, she stayed anyway. Stayed because she felt trapped and alone. She stayed and hid the truth about their marriage from herself. What they had was no longer a marriage. It hadn't been a marriage in years. This horror show she was in had become a prison sentence that Jude didn't think she could survive.

When Jude looked in the mirror now, she saw a shell of her former self staring back at her. The abuse and the constant stress were taking their toll on her, eating away at both her body and her soul. She'd lost weight that her 5'5", 120 lb. frame couldn't afford to lose. Her hair, once dark brown and shiny, was beginning to gray and thin. It had even begun to break off and fall out in small clumps. Her skin, which had once been smooth and glowing, was now pale and creased with worry lines. Jude was still in her early thirties, but she felt at least twice that age now.

She wanted to escape, to run away without ever looking back. But how could she do that? She didn't have anything, not a penny to her name. She didn't work. She was a professional housewife living in constant fear.

She didn't have anything that Tony didn't give her, including money. He gave her just enough to shop with, and he always checked the receipts and confiscated any leftover change. He barely allowed her to leave the house, and he demanded that she keep her phone's location and "find my phone" settings on at all times. He routinely checked her phone and computer activity. She didn't have access to his bank accounts, and of course, she didn't have an account of her own.

Jude often thought about reaching out to her family and friends for help. She wanted to tell them the truth about her life instead of hiding behind the occasional "Tony approved" text messages, emails, or phone calls where she pretended to be happy. She desperately wanted to call her family and friends and beg them to help her, but fear and shame always stopped her. She was a prisoner in this life, and Tony was the warden who had thrown away the key.

CHAPTER 24

Today's forecast called for rain, and as she stepped outside, Jude could see the thick, gray clouds moving in overhead. The sun was absent, but Jude wore her oversized sunglasses anyway. Makeup alone wouldn't cover her black eye and other bruises, no matter how much she caked on her face.

Jude descended the stairs leading from their second-floor apartment and silently prayed that she wouldn't run into any of their neighbors. The salty bay breeze blowing in off of the Chesapeake stung Jude's bruised skin, but she was still happy to get out of her dungeon.

"Good morning, Henry," Jude said, approaching the produce stand just outside of her apartment complex. The kind, old man always offered fresh fruit and a warm smile, and one of Jude's few joys was visiting with him.

"Good morning, Ms. Judy, and how are you this fine day?" Henry said as he turned towards the sound of her voice. "I have mango, passion fruit, and sweet yams, all fresh and just for you."

"I'm well," Jude lied and bent to pat Crisfield, Henry's "seeing eye" German shepherd. "Morning, Cris. How's my baby boy?" The dog wagged his tail and licked her palm.

Henry had remembered her since the very first day she'd visited his stand after Tony had moved them to Chesapeake Beach. He never once confused her with any of his other customers.

She stood and chatted with Henry for just a few minutes, mindful that she shouldn't spend too much time outside. After paying for her fruit and vegetables, Jude patted Henry's hand and said, "See you soon, Henry. Thank-you."

He gave her a slight smile and said, "No, you won't, Ms. Judy."

Surprised, Jude said, "What do you mean? Are you going somewhere, Henry? Are you taking a vacation? Wait, oh no, you aren't closing, are you?"

Henry's smile faded, and his brow furrowed behind his dark shades. He removed the cap he was wearing and rubbed his hand through his gray hair.

"I know what he does to you, Ms. Judy. And I hear the pain in your voice. For once, I'm glad my eyes no longer possess sight for fear of what they would see."

"Henry, I..." Jude began, but Henry held up a hand to cut her off.

"Please, just listen, Ms. Judy. I'm sorry and I don't mean to intrude, but I have fear in my heart. Fear for you, Ms. Judy. Fear that you won't survive if you don't save yourself. My baby sister had a husband like yours once."

Jude fell silent.

"We all knew what he was doing to her. Even called the police on him, but she refused to press charges. He even put her in the hospital a couple of times, but she lied about the cause of her injuries. We begged and begged her to leave him, but she always refused. Said he would take their kids if she left. So, she stayed. She stayed and cut herself off from our family," Henry said. "She stayed with that evil man. Stayed until one day, he killed her."

Jude remained silent, unable to speak at all now.

"They put him in jail, but it came too late. The kids are ok, they live with us now, but my sister is still gone, and those kids will grow up knowing what their daddy did to their momma. She's dead, and ain't nothin' going to bring her back."

Tears rolled down the dark, creased skin of Henry's cheeks as he said, "Ms. Judy, I don't want the same thing to happen to you, but you can stop this. Please stop it, Ms. Judy, for your own sake. Please get yourself away from that monster before he sends you to your grave."

CHAPTER 25

Jude crashed to the ground, her body slamming hard into the kitchen's linoleum tiling. Pain flooded her entire body as she felt the breath rush from her lungs. She was being punished again. This time because dinner was late.

"What is wrong with you, Jude?!" Tony yelled, his words liquor-laced and slurred. "Why do you make me do this every time?"

Jude scrambled to her feet, Henry's words from earlier echoing through her mind. *No, you won't...get yourself away from that monster.*

She limped into the bedroom, locking the door behind her. She could hear Tony's heavy footsteps coming down the hallway.

"Jude!" He began pounding on the door. "Open this goddamn door!"

Frantic now, Jude grabbed for one of Tony's pistols. She'd just removed it from the lockbox when the bedroom door exploded inward, flying off its hinges.

"What the hell did I tell you, Jude?" Tony yelled. "Now, you get your ass in there and clean that mess up! Right now!"

Jude mustered courage that she had believed she no longer possessed and rose to her feet, the gun shaking in her hand at her side.

"No, Tony."

"Bitch, what did you say?" Tony said, his barrel chest heaving in anger, thick veins pulsing in his large neck and arms. She could smell the liquor on his hot breath.

"I-I said no, Tony," Jude stammered. She raised the .38 and pointed it at his chest. "I won't let you do this to me anymore."

Tony's initial look of shock at the sight of his gun in Jude's hand turned into a malicious smile.

"You going to shoot me, Jude?" he growled. "You have the balls to point a gun at me, bitch?"

"Tony, don't," Jude said and cocked the hammer on the gun. It quivered in her hands. "Just leave me alone."

Undeterred, Tony took a step towards her.

"Tony, I said stop!" Jude said and put her finger on the trigger.

"What's wrong with you, Jude? You better put that damn gun down. *Now!*"

"You are what's wrong with me, Tony!" she screamed at him.

"*Look at what you've done to me.* I won't let you keep beating on me. I loved you, Tony. I've been a good wife to you, and you treat me like a damn dog."

Tony stopped and raised his hands. "Jude, now just wait a minute. Put the gun down and let's just talk about this, ok?"

"*Shutupshutupshutupshutup!* Get out before I kill you. *Get out!*"

"Jude, you better..." Tony said and started to reach one of his beefy hands towards her.

"Get out, Tony! Get away from me!"

She closed her eyes and felt her finger squeeze the .38's trigger.

The gun boomed twice, the loud noise surprising Jude. She felt the revolver jump in her hand, and she almost dropped it.

When she opened her eyes, Jude saw the two holes in the closet door behind Tony.

"Are you crazy, woman?!" he yelled. He'd dropped to the floor and cowered away on his hands and knees to the far corner of the room. For all of his bullying and abuse, Tony Landry was just a coward who wasn't ready to die.

She thought about dialing the police to press charges and have this bastard thrown in jail. But Tony was a policeman, and Jude didn't trust that they would turn on one of their own. They wouldn't do that, would they? No, they wouldn't.

As soon as Tony fled the apartment, Jude began packing her bags. The fear that had once paralyzed her was gone, replaced by a desperate need to survive. With speed and strength that she didn't know she possessed, Jude pushed the bed aside, pulled back a couple of loose floorboards, and reached into the hiding space that Tony thought was a secret. She removed the two large, plastic-wrapped stacks of cash that she'd always known was there but had been too afraid to even think about touching. She wasn't scared anymore, and she wanted out of this hell.

She placed the cash, the gun, and some extra ammunition in her bag as she gathered the last of her things. She dropped her cell phone in the toilet. She would buy another one. Jude rushed from the apartment using the building's fire escape so as to avoid her neighbors and the police who would be gathering out front by now. She didn't know where she was going, but she knew she couldn't stay here another night, not even another minute. She would leave this hell and never come back.

The next morning, after she checked out of her hotel room and just before she left town, Jude visited Henry at his fruit and veggie stand.

"Thank-you, Henry," Jude smiled through her tears. "You saved me."

"No, you saved you. You decided to stand up to him. All I did was call the police when I heard the gunshots. No one could've done anything until you made that decision." Henry smiled, "And now, your new life is calling, Ms. Judy. Are you ready to answer?"

"Yes, Henry, I'm ready," she said as she kissed him on his cheek and squeezed his hand. She stooped and patted Crisfield on his head and allowed the dog to lick her face and hand.

Jude knew the police wanted to speak to her, but she wasn't interested in dealing with them. Tony would cover it all up anyway to protect himself and his job, and his co-workers would help him. She just wanted to get as far away from here as possible.

Maybe she would head home to Seattle or maybe she would go somewhere and start over on her own. She wasn't sure yet, but she would find out. Jude's life was calling, and although she didn't know where it would lead her, she was going to answer.

PART SIX

"DONE IN THE DARK"

CHAPTER 26

Jacobs and Landry were ending their shift as they usually did on most days, camped out at their favorite dive bar. Torch's Alehouse and Grill was a longtime fixture on the Northeast side of the city, sitting just a few blocks from the precinct. Situated between South Dakota Avenue and Bladensburg Road, Torch's was a favorite haunt for cops, firemen, and the city's other emergency response workers.

Patty and Pete "Torch" McCaffery, the husband and wife owners of the bar, had opened up the place after Pete retired on medical disability from the Metro Fire Department and Patty retired from the D.C. government. The couple was friendly and welcoming and treated all of their patrons with a smile, open arms, and great service. They even allowed their most loyal customers to run up the occasional tab. Best of all, Torch's was a place where a cop could come and unwind in peace after a long, tough shift.

"Can you believe that bullshit today with Cole?" Jacobs started in again on the same topic he'd been harping on all afternoon. "That damn rookie gets our bust, solves our case, and gets to be the hero today. What kind of shit is that, Land?"

When his partner didn't answer, Jacobs took that as his cue to keep right on talking.

"I mean you talk about a shitty day, huh partner?" Jacobs said and downed the last of his drink. He threw up his hand and signaled for another. "We're the top dogs of this precinct, and everyone knows that. Who the hell does Cole think he is anyway?"

"Dumb luck, I guess," Landry mumbled. "What do they say? Sun shines on a dog's ass once in a while, right?"

"Dumb luck is right. Lucky bastard is what he is. That boy wouldn't know good cop work from his asshole, Land. No way. Am I right, partner?"

"We don't even know yet if he got the right guy," Landry said. "The punk that Cole busted spent most of the afternoon swearing he didn't have shit to do with the Mooney shooting. Said he was just puttin' on a show for his homeboys. Then he lawyered up. So, right now, it's just an arrest, Jake. Don't mean shit."

"Shit, it's a helluva lot more than the two of us got so far. A couple of our brothers gunned down and all we got for our end is exactly dick."

"Yeah" was all Landry offered as a reply.

"And Slick," Jacobs continued, shaking his head. "My God, man! What's the world coming to when a man like Slick Mooney can get gunned down in cold blood like that?"

"I hadn't heard you mention him in a while," Landry said. "Didn't know he was still around."

"Yeah," Jacobs said, his words catching in his throat. "Yeah, ol' Slick was still around. Things got rough for him after his wife passed away. He drifted away a bit after he left narcotics, but we kept in touch."

Jacobs felt a heaviness settle deep in his chest, a dull aching as he recalled the memories of his dead friend. Over the years, he and Slick had put in some damn good cop work together. Yeah, ok, so maybe it hadn't all been above board, but they brought down a lot of bad guys and even made a few coins for their retirement funds for their trouble. Too bad there wouldn't be any retirement for Slick now.

The news of Slick's murder hit him like an iron fist when he first heard it, but he'd changed that sudden pain and sadness into anger and a hard resolve to bring Slick's killer to justice. And he would do just that.

"Man, I tell ya, Land, Slick was a great cop. A cop's cop, ya know? Great man, too. And some sonofabitch chopped him down. Just like that. You best believe that when we get another crack at that Watkins kid, I'm gonna break his ass. Hear me, Land? I'll break him. For Slick."

"I hear ya, partner," Landry said, not making eye contact with Jacobs. "I hear ya. You'll break him for sure."

Jacobs and Landry had grabbed their usual table in the rear of Torch's with their backs facing the wall so they could see who came and went. They were currently on their third round of Johnnie Walker Black and ginger ale and Marissa, the evening shift waitress for Torch's, was bringing over their next round like clockwork.

As she approached, Jacobs looked her over from head to toe. He let his eyes linger over her best parts, which to him, was every, single inch. Her dark chocolate skin and long, thick, powerful-looking legs. The way her hair, brown with auburn streaks, was always freshly-styled in those perfect curls. The intensity of her light brown eyes, the shine of the lip gloss on her pouty bottom lip, the bounce in her full, perky breasts, and the sway of her ample hips. All of these things combined to make Marissa a gorgeous brick house of a woman who made Jacobs weak in the knees whenever he saw her.

As he always did, Jacobs allowed his mind to wander to thoughts of how Marissa was in bed and what he could possibly do to find out. He felt a twitch in his groin and his mouth began to water. Marissa was a student at nearby Trinity University and working at Torch's helped her pay her tuition. Maybe money was the right angle for him to get in between those magnificent thighs.

"You boys alright?" she asked and flashed her 1000-watt smile. "Four rounds in just an hour and a half. Damn, you boys are on it hard tonight. Rough day at the office, huh?"

"The roughest, honey," Jacobs replied with a smile of his own. "But, hey, what's new, right? Just keep 'em comin'. So, how's school going? Tuition not gettin' the best of you, is it?"

"Sure thing, sweetie," Marissa said. "School is school, you know. It's going. And bills are bills.

Always high and always due, but I manage." She winked at Jacobs, touched his arm and turned to leave.

Jacobs took a long stare at her perfectly round ass as she sauntered away. That masterpiece had its own rhythm and bounced however it wanted like it had a mind of its own. *Jeeeezsus*...he bet she was a monster in the sack. What he wouldn't give for just one night to find out...just one. He was sure he'd give a pinkie finger and a pinkie toe for that ride.

Shit, who was he kidding? What would a stallion like that want with his old, crusty ass? She had her choice of men for sure, and Jacobs didn't have that much money anyway. Hell, he spent most of his check and most of his "off the books" money paying bills and drinking his life away in this place. He was barely able to put anything away for himself, and he wasn't about to touch his emergency stash, no matter how fine the piece of ass.

He let go of his pipedream and returned his attention to his drink. He'd finished his third and was about to start on the newest round when he noticed Landry was still nursing his last drink. He'd hardly touched it, and the melting ice had caused the glass to sweat and the drink's color to fade from a golden-brown to something like a watered-down yellow. Landry gripped the glass and turned it around and around on the table.

Jacobs watched him for another few seconds before asking, "Hey partner, what's up? You goin' light on me tonight or what? You been babysittin' that drink for so long that I'm about to lap you, man. Where you at tonight?"

Landry didn't answer right away, and Jacobs knew to just wait. His partner of the last six years didn't say a whole lot most times, but the two men had covered a lot of ground during their time together and had come to understand one another.

After a few minutes of silence, Landry sat the drink down and looked at Jacobs with a deep sadness in his bloodshot eyes and a frailty Jacobs had never seen in his partner before.

"She left me, Jake. Jude left me. Left me high and dry. Gone," he said, his voice flat and low. "Bitch left me. Ten years of marriage, and now she leaves me."

Landry's confession caught Jacobs off-guard and caused him to sit his own drink down. *Damn.* He knew something was bothering his partner, but he thought maybe he would say something like one of his side chicks was having another pregnancy scare or something. He didn't expect to hear this. He guessed he shouldn't be surprised, but damned if he wasn't surprised. He hadn't expected to deal with this heavy shit tonight.

Jacobs knew that Landry and his wife had been having issues. His partner hadn't been a model husband over the years and wasn't exactly up for a husband-of-the-year award, but what cop was? That was part of the job.

Cops were married to the job more than they were their wives, but shit. Ten years of marriage was ten years of marriage. You didn't just walk away from that. But these days women did walk away, didn't they? Jacobs knew this and had two ex-wives and two kids of his own to prove it. They all hated his ass and saw him as nothing more than their monthly source of coin.

"Christ, bud," Jacobs said. "I'm sorry, man. Is she gone for good, you think? Something happen between you two? She find out about some of your extra-curriculars?"

"Man, I think she always knew about the other women, you know? And I kept doing it anyway. Now she's gone, man," Landry said as he wrung his hands together in front of him. He'd gone back to staring at his drink. "I went home, and all of her stuff was gone. Guess she's finally had enough of my shit, ya know?"

"Land, listen, don't beat yourself up over this. Ain't right for any woman to up and leave her husband like that, especially a cop. Shit just ain't right."

"Yeah, well, she's gone and I don't know where. She left her cell phone, and her mom claims not to know anything. I even called a couple of her nosey-ass friends, and none of those bitches were any help."

"Well, partner, you know what I say? When you fall off of one horse, you need to get your ass up on another one and buck that bitch until she kicks you off." He laughed and tried to lighten the mood, but he was talking to himself as much as he was talking to Landry. Jacobs hadn't had a piece of ass since wife number two had left him last year. Not including the ass he'd paid for since then. He didn't count any of those.

Landry looked up from his drink and stared across the table at his partner. Jacobs wasn't sure if Landry wanted to punch him in the face for his remark or if he would just get up and leave.

"Hey man, I'm sorry if I..." Jacobs started to say. "I didn't mean to..."

"You're right, Jake," he said. "Hell, if she wants out, then to hell with her, right?"

"You're a good man, partner," Jacobs said, and he wanted to believe that he was telling the truth. "Any broad out here would be damned lucky to have your shoes sitting under her bed."

"Thanks, bro," Landry said and held up his glass, "Fuck it, right?"

Jacobs matched his salute with his own glass. "Damn right. Fuck it all. Here's to Slick Mooney, and here's to your newfound freedom. Now catch-up you slow-drinkin', baby-sitting bastard."

The two men clinked their glasses together and then proceeded to get themselves properly drunk.

CHAPTER 27

It was almost one in the morning when Jacobs and Landry stumbled out of the rear entrance of Torch's. They had gone through nine rounds in almost five hours before Torch sent them on their way. Patty and Torch were closing for the night, so the two men paid their tab, left a big tip for Marissa, and made their way towards their vehicles parked behind the bar.

Jacobs wondered what he should do now. He was worried that his partner would be tempted to eat his gun, so he'd convinced Landry to stay at his place. But now, as they left the bar, he doubted that either of them was in any shape to drive. The last thing they needed was to drive into a light post or off the road somewhere or even worse, run over some civilian.

They had definitely overdone it tonight, way past their usual. Maybe they could just sleep it off in their vehicles for a few hours. Get up early enough in the morning to shower and change clothes at the precinct. Even in his drunken haze, Jacobs feared the hangover he knew he'd have to deal with in the morning.

They were staggering their way through the dark alley that led from Torch's to where they'd parked their car when Jacobs saw Landry stop walking. His partner leaned his back against the brick wall of the building and swayed a little to his right. Jacobs thought he might have to catch him, but then Landry straightened himself up. His eyes closed, and he let out a heavy sigh.

"You good, partner?" Jacobs asked the man as he tried to control his own balance. "Damn lightweight, I tell ya. Come on, Land. What's the deal? You can't hang anymore?"

"No, no man, I'm good, I-" Landry started to say, but then he stopped talking and started vomiting. He doubled over and let loose a few violent heaves. Brown liquid spewed from his mouth and splashed at his feet and on nearby trashcans. Jacobs had wanted to at least move Land's tie out of the way, but it was too late for that. He would have to toss that one in the garbage.

"There ya go, buddy," Jacobs said and patted his partner's back. "Get all that shit out. Then we'll get you to your truck."

"She left me, Jake," Landry said between heaves, sounding on the verge of tears. "The bitch left me; hell am I gonna do now?"

"You'll be ok, pal, you will. Trust me on this one. It'll all work out," Jacobs said, trying to reassure his partner even though he didn't believe his own words.

Landry began heaving again and in-between heaves, Jacobs heard his partner sobbing and wondered how it had come to this. Two grown-ass men, decorated veterans of the MPD, in a stinky, dirty alley trying to avoid the rats and vomit splatter while they wallowed in their misery.

Jacobs hoped he wouldn't have to carry Landry's big ass. He could barely stand himself, and his partner wasn't exactly a little guy. He would have to figure something out if Landry couldn't walk because they couldn't stay in this filthy alley all night.

"Straighten up, Land," Jacobs said when it sounded like his partner didn't have any more vomit or tears left in him. "Let's get the hell outta here. We gotta be in the office early tomorrow so I can get to work on that Watkins prick."

"I can't go home, Jake," Landry said. "Can't do it." He was still doubled over with his hands on his knees. He was shaking his head, and Jacobs thought he might start crying again.

"It's all good, partner," Jacobs told Landry. "Like I told you already, you can just crash at my place tonight, no worries. Hell, you can hang with me for as long as you need to, dude. Let's just get the hell out of this funky ass alley, ok?"

Jacobs didn't want Landry staying with him, but he was trying to be there for the guy. Landry was his partner and all, but hell. Jacobs had his own problems, and he wasn't no damn marriage therapist. If Landry's wife had left him, then she most likely had a good reason.

And partner or not, Jacobs didn't like sharing his space. He also didn't need to deal with Landry and his crap right now. What he needed to do was focus on this case and cracking that Watkins kid. If he was their shooter, then Jacobs needed a confession. If he wasn't, then Jacobs needed to get back on the street and find the real shooter before that asshole shot another cop.

Landry slowly stood upright. He seemed to be pulling himself together.

"No, I-I think I'm alright, Jake. I can go on home", he said as if reading Jacobs' mind. "We both need to be up early so we can get back to work."

"You sure, partner?" Jacobs said, trying his best not to show his relief. "Because like I said, you can crash at my place; it's not a problem."

"No, no, I-I can make it home," Landry said, his words heavily slurred. He looked at Jacobs but didn't meet his eyes. "I'm sorry for losing it like that, Jake. I-I just feel like it's all coming down around me, ya know? Some psycho taking out our brothers one-by-one. Then, Jude up and leaves me. I-I just don't know what to do."

"Partner," Jacobs said, "you can't let this shit get the best of you. Some things we can't control, but some things we can. Like making sure we nail the right man for these shootings and then sending his ass to hell. No trial, no sympathetic jury bullshit. Just a bullet to the back of the dome and a grave with the catfish and the mud at the bottom of the Anacostia."

"Jake," Landry said, "you ever think about the things we've done? Some of the, you know, the really bad shit. The shit we don't talk about anymore?"

Where the hell is this going? Jacobs thought. *Hell is wrong with Landry? Is he losing his mind?* This wasn't the time to start feeling guilty about anything.

"Hell no, Land," Jacobs said, agitated now. "You hear me? *Hell no.* There isn't a damn thing to think about. We've always done what we needed to do to make this job work. To make sure we survive out here in this damn warzone. You know it's like the middle east out here in these streets. So, we do whatever it takes, right? That's always been our way. *Whatever it takes.* We need to bust some heads, we do it. And, ok, we collect a little tax here and there. So, what? We deserve that and more for risking our lives every day. I'm talking warzone combat type shit out here. So, don't go soft on me, Land. Not now, not ever. This is how we've survived all these years. You with me, partner?"

Jacobs hoped that Landry wasn't flipping out on him. You never know when someone is at their breaking point until it's too late and then they break, and they take everything and everyone down with them. Was there a chance that IA was onto them? Rat squad bastards. Had they somehow gotten to Land and made him turn snitch on Jacobs? Nah, no way. Jacobs couldn't believe that. *Come on, Land. Pull your shit together,* Jacobs thought as he studied his partner and waited on an answer from him.

Landry looked up at the nighttime sky and let out a huge breath that it seemed he'd been holding forever.

"You're right, Jake," he said. "Damn, you're right. I must be losing it, man. I don't know what the hell is wrong with me."

"Look," Jacobs said, feeling relieved that he seemed to have gotten through to Landry. He still wondered if there was something that his partner wasn't telling him. He couldn't worry about that right now, but he wouldn't forget it either.

"You can't drive like this, Land. I won't let you. Last thing I need is for you to end up in a ditch somewhere. Look here, there's a 7-11 right up the block. I'll stumble on up there, grab us a couple cups of java, the strong stuff. Straight black. We get that shit in us and we'll be good to go after that. Take just a few minutes. Hop in the front seat of your truck and sit tight, ok partner? I'll be right back."

Landry did what he was told without another word. He was in bad shape. Jacobs shouldn't have insisted on them going out drinking tonight, but it was their routine. So, he hadn't thought twice about it. Still, he should've picked up on this sooner. His partner had seemed a little off and preoccupied all day, like there, but not there at the same time.

But hell, two of their brothers were dead, so they were all off, right? Who wouldn't be rattled with this shit going on? Jacobs had chalked his partner's behavior up to that and put it out of his mind. He'd figured sticking to their routine would help them both take the edge off. He couldn't have known that Landry was dealing with this other crap.

Jacobs felt a wobble and a sway in his step as he left the alley and headed up the block. He needed the coffee just as much as Landry. The streetlights cast an ugly yellow tint on everything and made Jacobs squint as he walked under each one. Shit, how many had they put away tonight? Torch had to cut them off just so he could close down for the night.

As he walked, Jacobs thought about the case again. He didn't like Rome Watkins as the shooter. The ballistics hadn't come back on the weapons they'd found in his possession, but Jacobs had the feeling that they would come back clean for the cop shootings. No way could Cole make this kind of bust even with all of the luck in the world on his side. That useless bastard didn't know a perp from a pile of steaming dog shit.

No, it would be up to Jacobs to bring the shooter down. First thing in the morning, he would put the press on that Watkins kid. Force him to admit that he was full of shit. Wouldn't take much. He didn't want to go down for this. He'd just been frontin' for his homeboys like he'd said, or maybe some young piece of ass he'd been trying to snag.

After he broke the Watkins kid, Jacobs and Landry would be back on the street hunting this cop-killer. And they would get him, too. No question. Because he and Landry were the professional anglers in this department. They caught the big fish around here, no one else. And one way or another, Mayday Jacobs always got his man.

CHAPTER 28

Landry started to doze off as he sat in the front seat of his Chevy pickup. The copious amounts of alcohol they had consumed overwhelmed him and just about put him down for the count. His eyelids were heavy and felt like twenty-five-pound dumbbells. His neck had turned into rubber and had started to give way as his head rocked backward onto his seat's headrest. He was just about out when he heard a noise on the passenger side of his pickup truck. Landry forced his eyes open and called out, "Jake? That you? I hear you out there. It's too late for this shit, you prick."

There was no answer from Jacobs, but Landry heard the noise again. It sounded like a knocking sound. If this was Jacobs' idea of a joke, it was a bad one.

"I'm not too drunk to kick your ass, Jake. Knock this shit off and gimmie my coffee, man."

Again, there was no answer except for the sound, a *thunk-thunk-thunk* against his pickup truck's metal body. Landry pushed himself upright, unsnapped his holster and removed his service pistol. He wasn't in the mood for this, but ok. If Jake wanted to play games, then he could play, too. They would both see how Jacobs liked having a gun pointed in-between his eyes.

Landry ejected the magazine and the chambered round from his pistol and sat them both on the seat next to him. He just wanted to scare Jacobs, not accidentally shoot his partner in the face. He just hoped he didn't make Jacobs spill the coffee.

Landry leaned across his pickup's front seat with his gun in his right hand. Using his left hand, he grabbed the passenger door's latch and slowly pushed the truck's door open. When the door was about halfway open, he leaned his body out and pointed his gun towards the rear of the truck, expecting to see a wide-eyed, scared shitless expression on his partner's face.

"Gotcha didn't I, asshole?" he said. "Now, where's my damn cof-"

Landry stopped midsentence, frozen in place by what he saw. He'd expected to see Jacobs. Instead, he saw a figure dressed head to toe in all black and down on one knee, pointing a small pistol squarely at Landry's head.

"Hell is this?" Landry said just before his brain caught up with his eyes. "Oh shit. No, wait!"

And then, just like that, Tony "Big T" Landry didn't see or think anything anymore. The muzzle of the shooter's pistol flashed, and in the next instant a bullet exploded into Landry's forehead and blew out the back of his skull. Blood, brain matter, and bone fragments painted the inside of his Chevy's door, and Landry's miserable existence came to a swift end.

CHAPTER 29

When Jacobs returned to the alley carrying two cups of steaming hot coffee, he remembered those little red stirrers. He'd looked at them, but had walked right out of the store without grabbing any. Probably too occupied with thinking about this case.

Oh, to hell with it, he thought. *Not walking back up there. We'll just use our fingers or something.*

He'd underestimated how far the store was from the bar. After walking the four blocks up and the four blocks back on wobbly, drunken legs, Jacobs was out of breath and damn tired now. The soles of his feet throbbed, and sharp pains shot through his knees.

As he rounded the corner past the entrance of the darkened bar and back into the alley, he could see that the passenger door on Landry's pickup was open. It was dark, but it looked like Landry was lying out of the door.

Had he gotten sick again? Well, at least he hadn't lost it in the cab of his truck.

Jacobs moved closer, and as he did, alarms started going off in his head. Landry wasn't moving. The hairs on the back of his arms and neck stood up, and his gut told him something was very wrong here.

"Hey, partner," he called out, hoping that his instincts were wrong. "You sick again? Man, maybe you need to lay off the sauce for a while, ya know?"

When Landry didn't answer, Jacobs slowed down and took in his surroundings. There was sparse lighting coming from a couple of poorly placed streetlights at either end of the alleyway, and Jacobs was forced to squint as he scanned the alley.

Jacobs moved a little deeper into the alley and then, as he came upon Landry's truck, he froze in his tracks. Jacobs let the two cups of coffee fall from his hand as he drew his pistol. The cups of coffee hit the ground with a loud splash. Scalding liquid washed across his shoes and ankles, but Jacobs ignored the pain. He was fixed on the sight in front of him. He stood just a few feet away from the pickup now and could see Landry's lifeless body hanging out of the passenger side of his truck. A gaping, bloody hole sat in the center of Landry's forehead.

Landry's dead eyes were wide-open. His service pistol lay on the ground a few inches below his dangling hand. At the sight of his dead partner, Jacobs kicked into automatic, moving forward on unsteady legs as he swept his weapon from side to side looking for the shooter.

"Aw no, hell no, Land," he said as he came up next to the body. Out of reflex, he stooped and placed his fingers on his partner's neck, though he could clearly see from the man's empty eyes and the jagged head wound that Landry was dead. As expected, Landry didn't have a pulse.

Jacobs yanked his cell phone from his coat pocket and dialed the department's emergency dispatcher. When the line was connected, Jacobs yelled into the phone, giving the operator his badge number, his location, and the code for "officer down."

After the dispatcher confirmed the order and promised to send backup to his location, Jacobs disconnected the line and moved around to the driver's side of the Chevy. He assumed a defensive position that best allowed him to cover the alleyway. If the shooter was still here, Jacobs didn't want him getting the drop on him.

"Damn it, Tony. Damn it!" Jacobs said as he continued to watch the alleyway.

After about five minutes, Jacobs heard the sirens of his approaching backup. When he saw the flashing red and blue lights lighting up the alley, he stood from his covered position and stepped around to the rear of the truck to flag down his people.

He stared at Landry's body as they removed it from the truck and placed it in a black body bag.

Who did this to you, Tony? Who's doing this to all of us?

"Detective," Jacobs heard from behind him and turned to see Cole coming up the alley. He was the last person Jacobs wanted to see right now.

"What you doing here, shit-bird? Shouldn't you be out directing traffic or something?"

Cole didn't flinch at Jacobs' insults and looked as if he'd been expecting the rebuke.

"Just here to help, Detective," he said, sounding exhausted. "I got the call, and I got here as soon as I could. That's it."

Jacobs stared at Cole. He was sure he had something like a burning hatred in his eyes, and although he knew he shouldn't feel that way towards Cole, he didn't give a shit. Yeah, maybe Cole was just doing his job, but right now, Jacobs hated the whole world and everyone in it.

"Yeah ok, rookie," Jacobs said. "So, go ahead and help...if you can."

Cole looked around, taking in the scene before he asked, "So what happened?"

The stupid question almost caused Jacobs to lose it again.

"Hell's it look like happened? Somebody, probably that same asshole who's been doing this, gunned down my partner in cold blood!" Jacobs yelled and pointed an accusing finger at Cole's chest. "And that means you arrested the wrong perp, shit-bird!"

To his credit, Cole still didn't flinch in spite of the accusation. He walked around to the back end of Landry's pickup to get a better look at the scene.

"Did you see anything?" he asked. "You were with Landry tonight?"

Jacobs stared at Cole again, not answering.

"Look, Detective, we made an arrest on what I thought was a credible lead," Cole said as he pointed at Landry's body. "But if we didn't get the right guy, then let's get him before he does more of this shit."

"Yeah, we were doing our usual after work thing," Jacobs said, the venom in his voice dissipating some. "We hit it pretty hard tonight. We were trying to shake it off before driving on home. I had gone up the block to get us a couple of cups of coffee, and when I came back, that's how I found Landry. That asshole put a bullet in his head, Cole. Must have got the drop on him, but it looks like Land was at least able to pull his weapon. Maybe he got a shot off and hit the bastard. Wouldn't surprise me if he did. Land's a tough sonofabitch. He wouldn't go out easy."

Cole walked over and, using a gloved hand, picked up Landry's pistol. He sniffed the chamber and then checked for a clip.

"It's not loaded, and it hasn't been fired," he said and placed the weapon back where he'd found it. "There isn't even a clip in it."

Cole looked inside the cab of the pickup. He reached in and came back out with the clip from Landry's weapon. He held it up for Jacobs to see before placing it back inside the truck.

"What the hell?" Jacobs said, hearing the surprise in his own voice. "No way. Even as drunk as Landry was, no one should have been able to get the drop on him like this. No way in hell. And why wouldn't his gun be loaded?"

"Maybe Landry was passed out," Cole offered. "Maybe he was checking the gun or something, securing it and nodded off. I don't know, Detective. How long did you say you were gone?"

"Yeah, maybe. He was hammered and in pretty bad shape," Jacobs replied as he continued to stare at his partner's body. "I wasn't gone more than a few minutes; I ran up the block to get that damn coffee."

"I'm sorry about Landry. I know he was your guy and you two went way back," Cole said, and he sounded sincere. "I'll start working the street and traffic cams, see if we can get lucky on this one. Maybe we got some video or a picture of the shooter."

"Goddamn it!" Jacobs said, exploding in anger, "Goddamn it! I shouldn't have left him." He pounded his fists on the roof of Landry's pickup truck.

Jacobs could see the techs and other officers at the scene stop what they were doing to stare at him. He didn't give a shit. Let 'em look. His partner was dead, and it was his fault. He shouldn't have left Landry alone. But they thought they had their man in lockup. This was Cole's fault, too. His bullshit lead made them put their guards down.

Jacobs turned and moved towards Cole, closing the distance between them in two large steps. "Go to hell, man. And take your sympathy with you because I don't need that shit from you. Your bullshit arrest helped cause this shit. Landry and I were out here with our guards down because YOU had everyone thinking we had our shooter in custody. I told Landry that was some bullshit. I knew it was. Knew there was no way you cracked this case."

"Detective," Cole started to say, but Jacobs cut him off,

"Shut your ass up," Jacobs said and moved to within an inch of Cole's face, all of the venom from before back in full force. "You don't know shit, rookie. I'm going to catch this asshole. Me. That's how it's always been, and that's how it's going to be now.

"Like I said before," Cole said, "I made the bust that was there to make, Detective. If we got the wrong guy before, then let me help you get the right guy now. I want to help."

His voice was measured and calm, but his body had tensed and shifted into a fighting stance. His hands had balled into fists, and the muscles of his jawline bulged as he spoke.

Jacobs could see that Cole was trying to restrain himself. He could also see that the rookie wasn't scared of him. Somewhere deep inside of himself, Jacobs respected that about the kid. He would never admit it, but he admired that Cole showed no signs of backing down.

The two men stood in a stand-off for the next couple of minutes, squared-up and not moving. Their faces were so close their noses almost touched. Both men were clearly ready to throw down if it came to that, but Jacobs knew that wouldn't do any good. The kid had just been doing his job, but someone had just blown his partner's brains out. So, he wasn't about to cut him too much slack.

"Yeah ok, Cole," Jacobs said, ending the standoff. "You want to help? Well, you better because you owe Landry just like I do. We'll catch this bastard. He doesn't know the hell that's coming for him. Just try to keep up, alright? Stay the hell out of my way, and I'll show you how to do some real-world cop shit out here."

CHAPTER 30

He is emptiness and sadness…he is hatred…

Once upon a time, there were two little boys who had their dreams stolen. While one of the little boys faded away never to feel the warmth of the sun on his face again, the other little boy grew into a man full of rage and fueled by hatred, living every day and breathing every breath with a determination to set things right. He needed to make those who'd stolen those dreams pay for their sins.

And now that was happening. With each wrong he makes right, he gets closer to the absolution and peace he's sought for so many years. His brother was dead, and he didn't do anything to save him. He was weak then, but now he's strong, strengthened by guilt and fortified by the need to serve justice. Although he grows closer to his goal, the job isn't done. So, he cautions himself against growing too comfortable, against growing careless and sloppy, and most of all, against faltering. Some might say that what he's doing is wrong, but they haven't seen what he's seen. They haven't lived how he's lived.

CHAPTER 31

Cole watched as the department's CSTs continued to process the crime scene. He studied their slow, methodical movements as they walked the grid of the taped off area. They combed over every square inch in search of anything that would help the detectives find whoever was responsible for what had happened here tonight.

He wondered if they would find anything or if this scene would end up just like the Mooney shooting. The crime scene techs working that one had failed to find anything useful. So far, these techs were coming up empty.

They had released Landry's body so it could be transported to the city morgue for processing. Jacobs had said that Landry was in bad shape. Was he referring to the heavy drinking or had there been something else going on with Landry?

Jacobs had left the scene a few minutes earlier to notify Landry's next of kin, get a shower and change of clothes, and report to the LT. He'd directed Cole to stay at the scene in case the techs came up with something useful. More grunt work.

Cole had wanted to unload on Jacobs when the two men were standing nose to nose. But he'd been fully aware of the many sets of eyes that were all watching them, waiting to see if the two would go at it right in the middle of a murdered cop's crime scene. That wouldn't work out well for Cole. He'd known this to be true, and so he held his temper in check.

He also knew he should feel empathy for Jacobs, with the man just losing his partner and all. But he didn't care. He'd wanted to put the fat man in his rightful place, which was on his back and on the ground.

But Cole had to admit that some of what Jacobs had said was true. His actions had indeed led to Landry's murder. Anyone with experience processing a scene would be able to see that Landry's guard had been down, and he hadn't stood a chance. But what Cole didn't understand was why Landry's service weapon hadn't been loaded. That one would be hard to figure out.

Drunk or not, the man's weapon should have been loaded. Bad luck for him, but a stroke of luck for his killer.

Cole would also have to keep an eye on Jacobs and his temper. The man had lost two of his close friends in less than a week. If he had to bet, Jacobs was near his breaking point. His rep was one of fire and brimstone and heavy-handedness, and now it would be even worse. Jacobs would be out for blood trying to avenge his friends' deaths. Cole didn't give a damn about Jacobs' mental well-being; he just wanted as much advance warning as possible when the man snapped.

He'd wanted to be in the mix and now here he was, all the way in it. He was standing neck deep in this shit now. And to make things worse, he'd just committed to helping Jacobs hunt a ghost.

CHAPTER 32

Jacobs was done dealing with the bullshit on this case, and he'd had enough of this "by the book" crap. Going "by the book" had gotten Landry shot down in cold blood. Now two of his close friends would never know another day. They were dead and gone, and now Jacobs was going to do things the best way he knew how. He would shake this town upside down until the shooter tumbled out like loose change out of someone's pocket.

After he'd left Landry's murder scene, Jacobs had tried and failed to reach his partner's estranged wife. Not like she would give a damn anyway. From what Tony had told him, she'd left and wasn't coming back. Jacobs doubted that she would care about his death except for the benefits the insurance would pay out to her. She'd be set for life thanks to a marriage she no longer wanted to be in.

Ain't that a bitch? Jacobs thought.

Jacobs made his way home so he could shower, change clothes, and grab a coffee and pastry before heading back to the office. After briefing Lieutenant Hernandez, his first order of business had been to talk to Jerome Watkins. And just as Jacobs had suspected, Watkins was no more their shooter than that asshole Cole who had led them to Watkins in the first place.

Jacobs had just started in on the kid when he broke down and confessed that he'd made it all up trying to impress his friends. The little bastard had even pissed himself in the interview room. Hell, Jacobs hadn't even needed to beat the truth out of the kid like he'd wanted.

Of course, any suspect would deny their involvement, but Jacobs believed Watkins. He'd interrogated enough suspects in his time to know that this was no act. The kid had wannabe written all over him. He was small time at best. They would charge him on the guns and the drugs, but Jacobs knew Jerome Watkins wasn't their cop killer.

Jacobs also knew that somebody somewhere did know something about these shootings. No way they didn't. He would go through each one of his snitches, along with anyone else who'd been on his radar and force them to give him something.

After turning the Watkins kid over to the processing unit, Jacobs found Cole sitting at his desk working on reports.

"Your guy Watkins? Yeah, he was some bullshit. Just like I thought," Jacobs said as he stood across from the younger man. "A wannabe, that's it. Definitely not our shooter."

Cole looked up at Jacobs but took his time answering. After a few beats, he said, "Ok, Detective, so what's next?"

"Techs pick up anything from the scene?"

"Nothing yet," Cole answered. "They haven't found anything useful. No shells, no prints. We're coming up empty so far."

"Shit," Jacobs said and sat down on the edge of Cole's desk. "Same thing as with Slick. So, our boy's a careful one, huh? Ok, well everyone makes a mistake at some point. Let's go see if we can speed up that process."

"Speed it up, Detective?" Cole said. "How do we do that?"

"You'll see. Let's go, rookie. Time to hit the streets and talk to some people, see if we can run this asshole down before he hits another one of our boys. You know, do some cop work. No way we'll catch this guy sitting at our desks typing reports." Jacobs turned to leave and waved with his hand for Cole to follow him. "So, let's hit it, rook."

CHAPTER 33

When Jacobs said "hit the street," he meant it to be taken literally. As in Jacobs hitting the street with the faces and bodies of his snitches who were being less than forthcoming with answers to his questions. With Cole riding shotgun, Jacobs spent the entire morning and most of the afternoon visiting his long list of informants without making much progress. Each one claimed that they didn't know anything about the shootings. And with each dead end, Jacobs found himself getting more and more agitated, becoming a powder keg of rage on the verge of exploding.

One snitch, a dim-witted bag of bones meth-head named Stevie, chose the wrong time to crack a bad joke about the cop shootings. Jacobs knocked the man off his feet with an uppercut and then tried to toss the skinny bastard out of a second-story apartment window. Cole stepped in and managed to restrain him before he could finish the job. At Cole's insistence, Jacobs agreed to leave Stevie's rundown apartment, but not before he promised to pay the man another visit if the addict didn't turn up something they could use.

CHAPTER 34

At almost 9:00 p.m., Cole and Jacobs were coming up on the end of their overtime shift and were on their way back to the precinct. As the two men rode in silence, Cole found himself understanding how Jacobs had managed to close so many cases. He'd spent the entire day watching the older cop shakedown and brutalize snitch after snitch without producing any viable leads.

Cole was sure that Jacobs had cooked the books on some of his cases and had even gone as far as to falsify and plant evidence for the sake of getting an arrest and a conviction. He wondered how many innocent men and women Jacobs had put away just to fabricate and maintain his "super-cop" legend. Cole had already known the man was a piece of shit but watching him in action today cemented that thought.

As if he could read Cole's mind, Jacobs broke the silence and said, "You know, the job ain't always pretty. It just ain't. And it ain't always politically correct and shit, ya know? Sometimes, hell most times, you gotta get your hands dirty. Get down in the weeds with this shit. You feel me, Cole?"

Cole stayed silent and Jacobs continued, "I see you sittin' over there judging me, judging how I do things. Shittin' on my methods. You saw how I roughed up those zombies out there today, right? Too brutal for your taste, huh? Did I offend your delicate sensitivities? Well, good. I'm glad. Because see, you don't know these streets like I do. You don't know this job like I do."

As Jacobs stopped the car at a red light, Cole turned and looked at the fat man, "And what exactly is it that I don't know, Detective?"

"You don't know what it takes to get shit done out here because you haven't seen the brutality that this job dishes out on a daily basis like I have," Jacobs said, turning in his seat to face Cole. "You're still new to this shit. Baby-shit green, in fact. Wide-eyed and innocent and all that crap. Yeah, I was like that once. Then I grew the hell up because I wanted to live and not end up with my head blown off in some alley like Landry."

Cole didn't bother to reply, and Jacobs returned his attention to the road as the light turned green and he started the car moving again.

After a couple of minutes of silence, Jacobs turned again to look at him, his narrowed eyes holding a bitterness that came from being on the job too long.

"You reading me, rookie?" he said in a low growl. "You hearin' what I'm saying to you? It's all about survival out here. To hell with justice. That shit is for the movies. It's about keeping *us* safe from those animals who are out there trying to take over. Any of this registering with you, Cole?"

Cole turned and met Jacobs' hard stare with one of his own and said, "No, Detective, I'm not reading you because I'm not like you. You can justify your actions out here all you want, but we both know that how you do things makes everything worse. Like you said, this isn't the movies. And like I said, I'm not you and I won't let the job change me into something that I won't be able to face in the mirror."

To Cole's surprise, Jacobs laughed then. A harsh, sarcastic laugh.

"Well, then you won't survive out here, rookie. You're already as good as dead. Better for you to eat a bullet right now by your own hand instead of prolonging the inevitable. This job changes you whether you want it to or not. Best to embrace that change and become whatever you need to become to survive out here in this jungle. If that means being an animal to deal with these animals, then so be it. I'll be an animal."

"Yeah," Cole replied, "you keep tellin' yourself that, Mayday... if that's what helps you sleep at night."

Without slowing down, Jacobs jerked the wheel hard to the right and steered his car into the precinct's parking lot. He jammed down hard on the brakes, causing the car and both men to fall forward and then rock backward in their seats.

Jacobs hit the button to unlock the car's doors without bothering to look at or speak to Cole again.

Instead, he jerked his thumb towards Cole and said, "Get your ass outta my car, rookie. You don't have what it takes to get shit done out here. You don't bleed blue. You'll never be true police, that's for sure. I'm sure you buy-in to all that bleeding heart, liberal bullshit, too. Hell, I bet you sit down when you piss. You're a liability out in these streets, and I don't need someone like you watching my back. I'll tell the LT to put you elsewhere. Let you sort out the paperwork or some shit. That's more your speed, not this out here."

Cole exited the car without another word. He watched as Jacobs' car sped off before he could even close the passenger door. The vehicle's back tires kicked up a cloud of dust and gravel as the car fishtailed its way out of the parking lot.

Cole looked at the car's taillights until they disappeared around the block. Jacobs was a walking train wreck just waiting for derailment. Cole thought to himself, *I think you're the one that has it all wrong, Detective. I'm not the one prolonging the inevitable.*

CHAPTER 35

After he'd kicked Cole out of his car, Jacobs had wanted to go to Torch's and drown his sorrows in drink, but he couldn't bring himself to do it. Not tonight. Not without Landry.

Not for a while, he thought.

He would've loved to get a look at Marissa, maybe chat her up a little bit. Gazing at that perfect ass would've been the perfect cure for all of his ills tonight. At least temporarily anyway. He just needed to take his mind off of things. But no, no Torch's tonight. It just didn't feel right, and besides, he didn't want to deal with the "I'm sorry for your loss" and "Hope you catch the SOB responsible" crap.

So, instead of going to Torch's, he stopped at a nearby liquor store and bought a bottle of Johnnie Walker Black and a bottle of ginger ale. Then Jacobs made his way towards the industrial park where Slick Mooney had been killed. Not the best choice of location given his current mental state.

To hell with it, he thought. *I'm drinking for Slick and Big Tony tonight.*

Jacobs steered his dark blue unmarked Crown Victoria into the parking lot near the abandoned buildings. He slowed the car to a crawl as he came upon the area cordoned off by the long strips of yellow crime scene tape.

How had this happened? How did Slick Mooney, of all people, end up gunned down while keeping watch over a bunch of old, abandoned buildings? He was better police than that. He'd been part of the elite, just like Jacobs. No way some mope should've gotten the drop on him. He should've never been working that bullshit post in the first place. Jacobs never understood why Slick had decided to retire just to end up pulling the night shift as a glorified security guard. Jacobs had plenty of questions, but not one damn answer.

He thought about his own life. How he'd let himself go to shit over the last few years. The daily drinking and weight gain. He was as big as a house now. Jacobs bet that he'd easily put on fifty, sixty, maybe even seventy pounds since he'd joined the force. Maybe more. The job will do that to you if you let it, and Jacobs had definitely let it.

The job will do other things to you, too. He and Slick had done a lot of bad things over the years. They had done things they weren't proud of, things they wanted to forget, things they had both sworn to never mention again.

Some of it in the name of the job. But the other stuff? He couldn't explain why he'd done those horrible things. He tried his best to block out the memories and to suffocate and bury that darkest side of him.

But the worst of it never goes away, does it? Some demons refuse to die. They cling to you, become part of your soul, and stay with you the rest of your life. No matter how many lies you tell yourself. No matter how much you try to drown it in drink. No matter how much you try to cover it with good deeds. Not that he'd ever done many good deeds himself.

He wondered if the demons had eaten away at Slick the way they'd eaten away at him? The two men, once thick as thieves, had drifted apart over the years. Now, his old partner was gone.

Jacobs pulled his cruiser just past the edge of the square created by the yellow crime scene tape and shifted the car's transmission into park. There was a chill in the air, but Jacobs was hot, and he rolled down all of the windows in his car to let the cold nighttime air fill the inside of his car.

He removed his liquid dinner from its brown paper bag and cracked the seal on the bottle of whisky. He put the bottle to his lips and took a long pull. The dark brown liquor tasted good and gave a slight burn as it passed over his tongue and eased down his throat.

Jacobs then reached over to the passenger side of his car and opened the glove compartment. He removed one of the blue Solo cups he kept in there. He noticed that he was running low and made a mental note to pick up some more cups before he ran out. He poured a generous amount of the Johnnie Walker into the blue plastic cup. Then he twisted the top off the bottle of ginger ale and poured a couple of splashes of it into the cup. He used his left index finger to stir the mix, and then he took a deep swallow from the concoction.

He exhaled a long, weary breath and said out loud, "Oh yeah. Now that's good shit right there. Exactly what I needed."

His thoughts drifted back to Slick Mooney and then to Tony Landry as he plowed through the

Johnnie Walker. By the time he'd finished half of the bottle, the pieces of this case had begun to fall into place for him. Slick and Land were both connected to him. Could their murders also be tied to him?

Jacobs thought about all of the wrong he'd done throughout his career. Wrong that he'd justified as right in the name of the law, but deep down, he'd known that some of the shit he'd done just wasn't right. Could all of this be his fault? Did Slick and Tony die because of *him*?

Was the killer someone from his past who was out for revenge? Did that mean he was next? He hadn't allowed himself to consider any of this before. His blown-up ego, he supposed; because in his mind, who would have the balls to come after Mayday Jacobs?

But now, with the Johnnie Walker guiding his thoughts, it all seemed to make sense. This cop killer could easily be someone from his past coming back to get him. Someone he'd wronged or sent up? Maybe even the family member of someone he'd put in the morgue. But wait, what about the cop who'd been killed before Tony and Slick? Jacobs didn't know him, so how was he connected to all of this? He would have to take a closer look at this entire case, all of it, from the very beginning. This whole time he'd been looking at this all wrong. Not connecting the damn dots.

Stupid Jake, he thought. *Come on, man, you're better than this. You should've been able to put this together...*

His thoughts were interrupted when he saw a flash of movement in his driver's side mirror. It was dark out and his vision was blurred, but he'd seen something move fast behind his car on the left side. Startled, Jacobs dropped his cup and the lukewarm liquid spilled in his lap, soaking the front of his tan slacks. For a hot second, he thought maybe it was a rat or even a homeless person. But if all of his years as a cop had taught him anything at all, it was to never take anything for granted.

CHAPTER 36

"Hell no, not me. Not tonight," Jacobs thought to himself. He started to reach for his Glock, but the alcohol had done its job. His fingers fumbled as he tried to free his weapon from its holster.

"Don't do it, Detective," he heard a man's voice say from behind him. "Your drunk ass will be dead before your fingers can even grip the butt of your weapon."

Then Jacobs felt the hard, cold metal of the business end of a pistol pressing against his skull just behind his ear. That sensation was followed by mind-numbing pain as the man delivered a hard blow to the side of his head. Stars flashed behind his eyes, and Jacobs felt his body give way as he slumped onto his side in a daze. When Jacobs opened his eyes again, he tried to sit up. His assailant shoved him back down, bringing on another wave of pain from his throbbing head.

Jacobs turned his eyes upward and got a blurred look at his attacker. The man standing over him was dressed in all black and wore a ski mask over his face.

"You know who I am, punk?" Jacobs asked, spit flying from his mouth. "I'm a goddamn cop."

"And that's why I called you detective, *Detective*," the man said, his voice muffled by the thick ski mask. "I know exactly who you are. Now hand me your weapon, butt first, and your car keys. And then place your hands on the steering wheel. Move slow."

Jacobs hesitated but then understood that he had no choice and did what his attacker commanded. The man snatched the keys and the Glock from his grip. He clicked off the weapon's safety and leveled it at point-blank range on Jacob's forehead. Jacobs thought about reaching for his backup pistol in his ankle holster, but the gunman seemed to be one step ahead of him.

"Go ahead and reach for it," the man said. "I want you to do it. *Please* reach for it."

Jacobs considered his options. He knew that he had none and left his hands on the steering wheel.

It occurred to Jacobs that the gunman knew he carried a backup piece but hadn't taken it because he wanted Jacobs to make a move for it, didn't he? As soon as Jacobs did, the man would kill him dead. But what if Jacobs didn't make a move? He was dead either way. Well, if he was going to die here tonight, he wouldn't go easy.

A police siren rang out and although it sounded like it was a few blocks away, Jacobs saw the gunman look in the direction of the sound as he tried to gauge the threat. Jacobs couldn't ask for better timing, and he thought that maybe now was his chance.

He leaned forward and reached for the small .380 he kept in his ankle holster. But once again, he was slow, and his attacker was ahead of the game and much faster on the draw. Without hesitation, the gunman raised the pistol he'd taken from Jacobs and brought the butt of the gun down hard against the top of Jacobs' head, causing him to collapse onto the floor of his car.

Pain roared through his skull again, and Jacobs could feel the warm blood running down his face from the fresh wound that had opened up on his scalp.

"You motherfucker, you!" Jacobs said as put his hand to his head. He felt the flow of warm blood seeping between his fingers. "Fuck you twice, you prick. You do what you came to do. Do the shit and get it over with. But you won't get far. My boys will hunt your ass down and there won't be no trial. You can believe that shit!"

The man took a step back from Jacobs and placed his weapon in the rear waistband of his pants, keeping Jacobs' own pistol aimed at him. With his left hand, he pulled the black ski mask up and away from his face. When Jacobs' vision cleared enough to allow him to see the man's face, he felt his mouth fall open in shock. If he hadn't known how this would end before now, what he'd just seen confirmed that it was all over for him.

CHAPTER 37

He is violence and vengeance walking...

The time has come to put an end to this madness. Right here, right now, this hell is coming to its rightful conclusion. The cop killer feels a surge of adrenaline as he tightens his grip around the pistol he holds. All of the rage and sadness that has taken up permanent residence in his heart now begins to shift and move him to finish this once and for all. All of the years he's been forced to wait. All of the sacrifices. He's tracked these animals, he's waited and watched from the shadows, and now he is making them pay for their crimes. What will happen next is the only form of justice he truly believes in. Jail will never be enough. The punishment should fit the crime, and it will tonight.

CHAPTER 38

Darius Cole stepped forward into the faint light of the fading street lamp flickering overhead.

Shock and confusion registered on Jacobs' face as his eyes grew wide, and he seemed to momentarily forget about the blood running down the side of his face. "C -Cole?" Jacobs said, his voice filled with disbelief despite what his eyes were showing him. "W-What the hell you doing, man? You did all of this? Y-You killed Landry? You killed those other cops?"

"No, actually, *you* killed those other cops," Cole said, his voice low and almost unrecognizable. "You don't remember me do you, Detective? It was a long time ago and well, you have done a whole lot of bad shit in your time, so I'll give you a pass on that one."

"Y-you killed Landry," Jacobs managed to say, still sounding as if he didn't believe what he was seeing. "Why would you do that?"

"Oh, your boy Landry? Yeah, he was a dirty cop like you. But you already knew that, right? He was a lot like you. You and he did a lot of dirt together, didn't you? Sent innocent men to jail. Ruined a whole bunch of lives. You both even got a couple of dead bodies on you."

Jacobs didn't respond, so Cole continued. "He was also a coward who beat the shit out of his wife like she was his human punching bag. A friend of mine hipped me to that situation. So, yeah, Landry got what he deserved. But truth be told, I gave him a break; because when it was his turn, he got it kind of fast. But you? You deserve to go slow. I suppose you're still struggling to remember me, huh?"

"Remember you how? What the hell are you talking about, man?"

"You took something from me. Years ago."

"What? Took something? What are you—?"

"It's been more than twenty years now," Cole said, cutting him off. "So, this has been a long, long time coming."

He could feel the tears beginning to well up and burn his eyes. He willed himself not to shed those tears. Not anymore. There had been enough of that over the years. "You and your partner stopped two little boys on their way home from school. They weren't doing anything. You just stopped them for no reason. Just because. You stopped us. We were on our way home, and you decided to mess with us. I was just a young boy, but I remember it all like it just happened. You took something from me that day. From my family. You ruined us that day."

"Wait. I, I didn't—" Jacobs tried to protest, but Cole waved the gun side to side causing Jacobs to abort his protest and fall silent.

"You did things to my brother. Things that changed him. He told me. He told me what you did to him. What you made him do...to you. How you...how you and your partner...took advantage of him...you beat him...y-you...you molested him...and then you left him with some stranger. Made him forget who he was. He was gone for two years. The things you and your partner did. Slick was his name, right? The things you did to him. You killed my brother that day. Even after he made his way back to us, he never truly came back. He was gone, and he stayed gone all the way up until the day he overdosed and died alone with a needle sticking out of his arm. See, because of you, my brother became an addict who spent his last day on this earth getting high in a dope house."

"Cole, wait, look. Listen to me, ok? I didn't...I didn't mean to," Jacobs said, his voice a desperate quiver now. "Look, I-I'm sorry, ok? I, man, I have kids, man. Please. Don't kill me, ok?"

After all of this time waiting and watching for the right time. After all of these years. Hearing the man responsible for so much of his pain begging for his worthless life now was all Cole needed to finish this once and for all.

He pulled his pistol from his waist and moved closer to Jacobs. He placed his weapon at the side of his head and put the barrel of Jacobs' pistol under the man's flabby, double chin.

"Cole, just wait a damn minute, ok?" Jacobs tried to say through gritted teeth. He began to sob, and fat tears rolled down his red, plump cheeks. "Please, just don't do this, please don't...do...this. Please, ...I-I'm sorry, ok? I don't, I don't want to die. Not like this. I'm a sick bastard and I know this but, we can work something out, ya know? Just tell me what you want, man, please!"

"I want you to heal yourself...heal us all...I want you to absolve yourself of your sins. I want to help you do it. I helped Mooney and Landry and now I'm going to help you." Cole kept his pistol to the side of Jacobs' head. He took Jacobs' pistol and offered it to him.

"Take it," he said, his voice flat and void of emotion. "Take your gun."

"N-no," Jacobs whined, "I don't want it. I don't want it. If you're going to kill me, then just do it, man."

He was a broken man now. But Cole wasn't finished making him pay yet. He whacked Jacobs hard on the back of his head again. Jacobs howled out in pain and started to fall forward, but Cole grabbed the back of his collar and pulled him back up.

"Take the gun," Cole repeated.

"Oh God, Cole, no, no, no, no." Jacobs yelled in between sobs, "Please don't make me do this. Please, please don't." He blubbered and shook.

"Either way you're leaving this earth tonight. This can go slow, hard, and painful by my hand or you can do the right thing and go fast by your own hand. Either way suits me just fine, but I gotta be honest with you, Detective. I'm really hoping you choose my hand."

Jacobs looked over at Cole. His eyes contained the same fear that Cole was sure his brother's eyes had held all those years ago while this monster violated him. The same fear Cole had seen in Beanie's eyes that day in the grocery store and almost every day after. This was what Cole had waited to see all of these years. This was what he'd needed to see.

With a shaky hand, Jacobs grabbed the gun.

"Now," Cole said, "Place it under your chin."

Jacobs did as he was told. His will to resist gone now.

"Now finish it," Cole commanded. "Finish what you started all those years ago."

Jacobs nodded, but then he hesitated and opened his mouth to speak.

"I...I'm sorry, Cole. I didn't mean..."

"Don't," Cole said through gritted teeth and pushed the barrel of his gun harder into the side of Jacobs' head. "Don't say that to me. You don't get to feel sorry for what you did."

Jacobs nodded and shuddered as he exhaled a large breath. His tears had halted and the fear had left his eyes, replaced by what appeared to be resignation and perhaps...peace.

Jacobs squeezed the trigger on his gun, and the pistol jumped in his hand as it delivered a bullet that blew out the top of his skull. Crimson splattered across the inside of the car, ruining the upholstery on the Crown Vic's roof and seats and staining the windows. Cole wanted to fire his weapon, keep squeezing the trigger until he heard the familiar clicking sound that signified an empty clip. But he knew that one round was all that was needed. Jacobs was dead and gone and on his way to hell...and the world was a better place now.

After it was done, Cole stared down at the body as it sat there, lifeless and unmoving, in the front seat of that car. Jacobs' head had fallen back against the headrest. His dead eyes were open, and a thin stream of smoke escaped his open mouth. A large hole had opened in the top of the man's head, and blood and brain tissue littered the inside of the car.

A wave of relief washed over Cole as he exhaled the breath he'd been holding in for more than two decades. The weight, heavy as an elephant, that he'd carried for most of his life fell off of his shoulders. But what he didn't feel was remorse.

He'd always wondered if he would feel any regret or sorrow when the time came. But now that it had happened, now that he'd done what he set out to do, he didn't feel any of that.

He hadn't done this for himself, he'd done this for Beanie. He'd done it for his heartbroken parents, but not for himself. He'd done it because he felt he owed this debt. He'd done it for his family and all of the other families that these men had ruined with their crimes.

Cole had made his way the best he could while his brother had continued his downward spiral. Somehow Cole had managed to avoid child services and foster homes by staying with a relative or a friend whenever he could until he legally became an adult. He'd put himself through school and had grown into a man, but the pain had refused to loosen its grip on him.

So, he'd sought out his pound of flesh, and now he'd gotten it. But as he'd expected, he didn't feel better about it. All he felt now was relief like his soul had been unburdened.

CHAPTER 39

Despite their fanfare and pristine arrest records, Slick Mooney, Big Tony Landry, and Mayday Jacobs had been far from the outstanding cops everyone had believed them to be. Cole had watched the three men. He knew what they were. They were monsters who had fallen from the ranks of the righteous years ago. He'd seen them shake down local business owners and drug dealers alike. He'd seen them rob and steal and abuse their shields. Most of all, he'd watched that day as Jacobs and Mooney had taken his older brother away to commit unspeakable brutality against him. And so, he'd waited until he could make things right.

After graduating from college, Cole set aside his dreams and chose a different path to combat his demons. He did a four-year enlistment in the Army, which included two combat tours—one in

Iraq and one in Afghanistan. But his demons persisted no matter how many insurgents he gunned down.

After the military, with his demons still alive and kicking, Cole tried again to bury them by living a "normal life" as a civilian. Find a quiet job, just be regular. But he soon reached a point where he could no longer outrun those demons, and he decided to face them head-on by going into the police academy and becoming an officer in the Metropolitan Police Department.

Then he'd waited and watched and worked, and then waited some more. Cole had waited until his opportunity came in the form of the first cop killing. And while he'd waited and watched, he'd seen Jacobs and Landry do much more harm than good. But not anymore. Now that was all over. His waiting had paid off, and he'd done what he had set out to do. He'd done this for Beanie.

Like he'd told Jacobs, Landry had been dirty and deserved the bullet, no doubt. But Jacobs and Slick Mooney had been monsters who'd gotten off easy. They both deserved a much worse death than what Cole had given them. Mooney and Jacobs had been the cops who'd taken and ruined his older brother. Slick Mooney had been the cop driving that day, and though he may have been eaten alive by the guilt towards the end of his career, he'd still deserved to die.

Cole had no idea who had gunned down that first cop, but his death had helped him and his cause. Whoever the killer was, he'd done Cole a favor by getting this whole thing started. He supposed it was someone who had grown tired like he had and decided to push back. Someone who had grown tired of seeing corrupt policemen go unchecked. Tired of the injustice. Or maybe they had just been tired of life's bullshit...all of it...and they had snapped and killed an innocent man. Who knew if they would ever catch the guy? He certainly wouldn't contribute to that effort. Hell, for all he knew, he would end up becoming the killer's next victim.

Maybe Cole had gotten a killer with his arrest of Rome Watkins earlier that day, and maybe he hadn't. He didn't give a shit either way. The kid had been lying about killing Slick Mooney. Most likely trying to build his street cred off of Cole's act of vengeance. Whatever else he was, Watkins had been just the cover that Cole needed to make his final play. Everyone had thought the killer was off the street and had let their guard down. Of course, now everyone would know that he hadn't gotten the shooter, but he couldn't worry about that. Bad arrests happened all the time.

Besides, he had bigger problems to worry about right now. He couldn't afford to let himself get caught. He'd just done the world a favor, but his fellow cops and the courts wouldn't see it that way. If he got caught, he'd be put away forever. He couldn't let that happen.

Cole wanted to get home, get a hot meal, and lay it down for the night. But first, he had a mess to clean up. He needed to canvass the scene and make sure there wasn't anything to link him to the scene. He'd planned this down to the last detail, but he'd known he would need some luck as well.

He'd gotten that luck with Jacobs drinking himself into a stupor hanging out in the same place where he'd gunned down Slick Mooney. He'd managed to catch up to Jacobs after he'd dropped him off. He'd spotted Jacobs driving near his normal drinking spot. Cole's luck kept rolling when Jacobs didn't go into the bar. Cole watched him buy his liquor, and then he'd followed him here.

By the time Cole had made his move, the streets had been just about abandoned. Someone would find the body in the morning, but he would be long gone by then. If questioned, his alibi would be that he'd been dropped off at the station by Jacobs. This had been true, and there had been plenty of cops around who could corroborate his story.

When Cole first planned this, he thought that when it was all done, he'd turn himself in and accept his fate...but why should he? He'd done a good thing today, right? He'd served justice and righted a wrong that had destroyed a family. And no matter what anyone else would think, this was justice. A righteous kill in his book. And now, after all this time, it was finished. He could quit the force now if he wanted. When asked about his sudden decision to leave the MPD, he could blame it on PTSD or something like that. Or maybe he could blame his leaving the force on the guilt of arresting the wrong perp, which had led to the deaths of two more officers. Some of this had the added benefit of being true anyway.

But if he quit suddenly, there would be questions. Jacobs and Mooney had been partners back in the day. Someone would find that connection sooner rather than later, and this case would gain national attention. Maybe the LT would keep him on the case, even make him the lead, and this would end up being the break he needed to get his career on track.

But that was a pipe dream, wasn't it? The reality was that this case was a career killer, not a golden opportunity. He was the shooter, and there was no way he would let himself get caught. If he was the lead, he would spend all of his time doing everything he could to steer the investigation away from himself. No, the LT should put someone else on this and let them chase their tails until this became a cold case. The best thing would be for Cole to transfer to another division. Narcotics maybe. Maybe even another precinct to get a fresh start.

CHAPTER 40

The next morning, at just past 7:30, Cole sat at his desk nursing his usual cup of green tea. His eyelids felt heavy and he had to stifle a yawn every few minutes, but his heart was at peace. When he'd made it home last night, he wolfed down a few pieces of leftover KFC and then he hit the sack for a few hours of sleep before getting up and heading into the office.

For the first time in as long as he could remember, he'd found sleep easily. The nightmares he'd expected, visions of his dead brother and the faces of the men he'd killed, had not haunted him while he slept. The past he'd allowed to dictate his present and future for so many years, had been put to rest for good.

Now Cole sat at his desk waiting on word of last night's killings. Jacobs' body would be discovered soon, and that's when all hell would break loose.

He'd just finished the latest round in his ongoing text message war with Sienna and didn't have much else to do now but wait. Sienna had started in early with her usual nastiness, but he was too tired to go back and forth with her today. So, he'd told her to go to hell, and then he'd blocked her number. When the call came at almost 8:30, it came as it always did, without warning and full of chaos. MPD officers and personnel began scrambling around trying to respond to the news that another one of their brothers was dead.

Lieutenant Hernandez, for his part, also didn't deviate from the script. He snatched open his office door, damn near pulling it off the hinges, his face colored into a bright shade of red as his voice boomed across the crowded room.

"Cole! Where the hell is Cole?" he shouted, his short arms waving in the air as he turned his head from left to right. After a couple of scans around the crowded room, the LT spotted Cole sitting at his desk near the back of the squad room. He pointed at him with a single fat finger and said, "Cole! My office, RIGHT NOW!" Then he turned and went back into his office, slamming the door shut behind him.

A few minutes later, Cole exited Hernandez's office, trying his best to suppress the smile that fought to spread across his face. *Probable suicide.* That was the M.E.'s initial classification of Jacobs' death. Not homicide, but probable suicide. Cole had tried his best to make the scene look like a suicide, but he'd had no way of knowing for sure if his plan would hold up under the scrutiny of the Medical Examiner.

The LT had been furious, and rightfully so. He'd just lost his two top dogs and was left with Cole and a few other overworked, underachieving detectives.

"A green, half-assed rookie," he'd called Cole, but Cole hadn't been offended in the slightest. He was happy to be thought of that way for now because it pretty much removed any suspicion from him.

The LT had chewed his ass about getting the wrong man and possibly costing two fellow officers their lives, but Hernandez hadn't truly been able to blame Cole for following a viable lead and making an arrest. As the head of Homicide, he was feeling the pressure and had sought to take out his frustrations any way he could. His career was on the line, and the heat from the chief, the mayor, and the public would be backbreaking.

The LT had even hinted at a possible Internal Affairs investigation into police corruption in their precinct, specifically Landry and Jacobs. Allegations had been made, but the LT had promised to fight any investigation by IA. No need to tarnish a dead man's rep, he'd said. Hernandez had dismissed Cole from his office, telling him to "go and do some paperwork or something."

There would be funerals, massive media coverage, and the ongoing investigation. The MPD would put on a public show of force, rounding up any and every one that could be their shooter. A few more lives would be lost during all of this. Eventually, the case would go cold, but there would be new cases to solve. And life would move on. Life would keep moving on until the next tragedy happened, and then it would move on past that one, too. Life was strange in the way it kept moving non-stop from one horrifying event to the next without missing a beat. This time wouldn't be any different.

So that's how this would play out. The young boy nicknamed Scoop had grown into a man and had exorcized his family's demons with "eye for an eye" retribution for the sins Jacobs and Mooney had committed against his brother. Now he hoped that his own dark past never came to light; but if it ever did, then he would deal with the repercussions.

After all of these years, Cole had to learn how to live an actual life, instead of just chasing a ghost. He'd decided not to quit the force. There was still plenty of good that he could do. And perhaps, maybe he could atone for his own sins. He still had bills to pay, and a crazy female to get rid of...for good this time, and a whole list of other crap to deal with...So, yeah, Cole still had problems to deal with, but setting things right for his brother and their family was no longer one.

EPILOGUE

"PEACE"

ONE

Interstate 80 looked as if it could go on forever. And that was just fine by Jude. She'd never been to Ohio and was enjoying the new view. The sun was out and the sky was a crisp, beautiful blue. There wasn't much to see in the way of scenery near the highway, of course, but what Jude was enjoying the most was fresh air, the freedom of the open highway, and the peace and quiet. She was at peace. Or at least on her way to it.

The first thing she'd done this morning after checking out of her hotel was to catch an Uber to a nearby car dealership. If the saleswoman had noticed Jude's bruises, she'd had the tact not to comment. She'd discreetly asked Jude if she needed any help, but after Jude declined, she left the subject alone. However, what she did do was make Jude an incredible deal on a five-year-old Toyota Camry with fairly low miles and shiny black paint. Jude was unemployed with no relevant credit history, so getting approved for a car loan had not been an option. But what Jude did have was plenty of cash. The saleswoman and Jude had reached some sort of silent understanding and she'd gone out of her way to get Jude into a car.

The saleswoman, whose name was Dana, applied every discount she could think of and managed to get the price below the $10k limit, which would require IRS reporting. After thanking the saleswoman and giving her a hefty tip, Jude had driven off of the used car lot with a full tank of gas in her freshly washed vehicle and a huge smile on her face.

Jude was driving home to Seattle. She hadn't notified anyone. She'd thought about calling her family but had decided against it...at least for now. She was sure Tony had called them and they would have questions that she didn't want to answer right now. She would call them in a day or so. Her first consideration for travel had been to fly, but the chance to make this trip over several days had been too much to resist. And so, Jude had packed her few belongings, including the cash she'd taken from her husband, in a couple of bags and had hit the road. She drove about eight hours before stopping at a hotel for the night.

The next day, as she was driving, Jude heard about her husband's shooting on the radio. He'd been killed in the line of duty. The police didn't have any suspects, but they were linking it to the other recent cop killings. Jude's chest had seized up when the radio announcer first broke the news. Her eyes blurred and she gripped the car's steering wheel hard to keep the car from swerving off of the road. Her first instinct had been to take the next exit and turn around. But she'd forced herself to keep driving. Tony Landry was no longer her problem. No longer her life. The bruises from her past life were still there, but in time, those would fade away too. The memories would take longer to fade, but Jude could live with that.

On her way out of town, Jude had purchased a new cell phone. After hearing the news, she briefly considered calling the precinct or even Tony's despicable partner but decided against both. Whatever happened, she was sure Tony had deserved it. Jude even silently thanked whoever was responsible for his death. Tears flooded Jude's eyes. She'd loved Tony once, but he'd destroyed that just like he almost destroyed her.

What happened next surprised Jude. Using the back of her left hand, Jude wiped the tears from her eyes and then...Jude began to laugh...out loud and uncontrollably. She laughed hard until her stomach muscles ached and new tears sprung from her eyes and ran down her cheeks. She was free. Jude was free, and she didn't have to worry about divorcing Tony or him coming after her. There would be questions from the authorities, they would want to rule Jude out. They would also question why Jude had left town so abruptly, but she would cross that bridge when she came to it. For now, Jude was going to make the most of her newfound freedom. She would enjoy the long car ride and hotel stays over the next few days and then, once she arrived in Seattle, she would begin plotting the next move in her new life. Tony Landry was dead and gone and Jude Landry was free. And that's exactly how it was supposed to be.

TWO

Today was a mild winter day by normal December standards in the Nation's Capital. The sun was perched high in a bright, cloudless blue sky and the temperature was a pleasant fifty degrees. Darius Cole steered his dark blue Nissan Maxima off Sheriff Road and through the gates of the National Harmony Park Memorial Cemetery in Hyattsville, Maryland. He'd been here many times over the years and knew his way by heart. He drove along the winding roads and small hills until he reached his destination.

Cole parked his car along the side of the narrow road and grabbed a plastic bag from the passenger side seat as he exited the vehicle. He crossed the road and began walking up the familiar hill he'd walked so many times before. Just over the crest of the small hill, Cole found what he was looking for. He kneeled in front of two graves. He brushed away the leaves from the nameplates and pulled at the weeds that had grown in since his last visit. He pulled two small bundles of flowers from the plastic bag he'd been carrying and placed one in each gravesite's flower holders. His father's and brother's graves were almost identical with the exception of the different names and dates on their small copper nameplates. Each gravesite was plain and barely noticeable among the more elaborate sites that sported large, ornately patterned headstones. The plots had been part of his father's plan for him and his mom, but they had buried Beanie here instead.

Cole spoke to his father first. "I did it, Dad. I took care of it. I told you I would. I-I'm sorry it took this long," he said and felt a knot tighten in his chest, "but I found the men responsible for destroying our family. And I put an end to those bastards. I put them down like I promised I would. Now you can rest."

He looked at his brother's grave.

"Beanie, I'm sorry this happened to you, bro. Sorry they ruined your life the way they did. But I tried my best to make it right, man. I know it won't fix anything, but at least those bastards aren't out here walking around, and they'll never hurt anyone ever again. I miss talking to you, man. I miss how things used to be. I miss our family. I just, I guess I just miss it all."

Cole looked up at the sky and then back down at the graves as he blinked away tears. "I'm not proud of what I did, but it needed doing, so I'm not sorry for it. I know I'll have to answer for those bodies in this life or after, but I can stand for it. And until that time comes, I'll keep helping people any way I can to try and make sure they don't go through what our family had to go through. I love y'all, man. And I hope y'all can forgive me."

Cole picked a few more stray weeds from his father's and brother's gravesites and whispered a prayer for forgiveness before turning and walking back down the hill towards his vehicle. He'd spent a lifetime trying to kill his family's demons. And now, he would close this chapter and begin a new one.

At long last, he...is...peace...

The End.

Author's Note

Darius Cole is a featured character in Bad Intentions *(2nd Edition). I wrote "Done in the Dark" to serve as a sort of prequel to Cole's story and to provide readers with more insight into his origins. If you enjoyed reading "Done in the Dark," be sure to catch more of Darius Cole in* Bad Intentions, *on sale now: www.scriptedvisionspublishing.com*

Thanks for reading!

Tyrone Eddins Jr.

Acknowledgments

First and foremost, I want to thank GOD and my Lord and Savior, Jesus Christ. ALL things are possible with Faith at the forefront.

Next, I want to thank my beautiful wife and partner, Janelle. I also want to thank my entire family: Dad, Mom and Mom, Uncle Gerald, my siblings: Danesha, Jason, and Marvin; my nieces, Daria and Daniella; all of my aunts, uncles, and cousins; the Zamores, the Duncans, the Moores, and everyone else that is part of our huge family tree. I love and appreciate each and every one of you!

I also want to thank the Fellas, the That's Game! Sports crew, and the Meeting of the Minds.

I also want to thank everyone that worked so hard to make Done in the Dark possible: Ms. Robyn Thomas, Dad, and Mr. Michael Zamore for the fantastic edits and incredible insight and Ms. Kedi Darby for the outstanding cover design.

If there is anyone that I have forgotten, please blame it on my crazy mind and not my heart.

Peace and Blessings,

Tyrone Eddins Jr.

www.ingramcontent.com/pod-product-compliance
Lightning Source LLC
Chambersburg PA
CBHW030808310726
48980CB00006B/423/J

* 9 7 8 0 9 8 5 0 6 6 6 3 5 *